My Name Is Not Devdas

My Name Is Not Devdas

A Novel

AAYUSH GUPTA

HarperCollins *Publishers* India

First published in India by HarperCollins *Publishers* 2022
Building No 10, Tower A, 4th Floor, DLF Cyber City, Phase II,
Gurugram – 122002
www.harpercollins.co.in

2 4 6 8 10 9 7 5 3 1

P-ISBN: 978-93-5629-282-6
E-ISBN: 978-93-5629-283-3

Typeset in 11.5/15.7 Minion Pro at
Manipal Technologies Limited, Manipal

Printed and bound at
MicroPrints India, New Delhi

To my special three, for putting up with me. I don't think anyone else could.

'...if true love breaks as easily as a delusion, on what can we rely? What will people pin their hopes on?'

'They'll have the sweet, intimate memories of a lost paradise, and beside it a sea of sorrow...'

—Saratchandra Chattopadhyay

Contents

1
THE INMATE

Devdas

Here on the Inside, *everything* mattered more—your name, your crime, your God. That's my summation.

Every great summation needs an example, so I'll give you one. For instance, on my last day, the inmates had asked my name. I told them, but I don't think I'll tell you. I am disinclined to make the same mistake twice. No offence, humans are untrustworthy and stupid. And for no particular reason, I shall labour under the impression that you are amongst those unfortunate enough to no longer be apes.

Anyway, my name, which I told them, meant more to them than it had to me.

'*Tui ki Ban-gaal?*' the smallest, meanest of them asked. *Were your parents, or their parents, or theirs—you get my drift—from Bangladesh?*

Now, I am a fairly intelligent person, more than most people. You could say I am almost an ape. That didn't keep me from baring my contempt.

'*Ami Ghoti.*' I declared with pride. No one in *my* family had set foot in that pseudo-Bengal, assured as we were of our worth through the many *da*s of the *true* Bengal. Manik da, Pancham da, Dada, collectively ingrained in me a self-belief usually reserved for religious nuts.

The other inmates didn't share my belief. They had plenty of their own.

'*Ami Ban-gaal*,' another Small One said. His tone was challenging. The Small Ones were always overcompensating.

I wrinkled my nose. They caught that, I am afraid to say. Almost immediately, a closed fist made contact with my left temple. Somehow, my feet gave way beneath me. My last memory was a foot swinging in a perfect arc, an arc that had my face in its trajectory.

In the right circles, a kick like that could have landed the foot a spot at Mohun Bagan. Here, it would do nothing but land me in the infirmary. What a waste.

The last sound I heard wasn't my nasal cartilage collapsing in on itself. It wasn't the light, appreciative laughter. It was,

'*Bhadralok.*' Gentleman.

Yes, that was me all right. And gentlemen have names. As a last service to my father, I shall refrain from mentioning mine.

Tell you what, my name is *not* Devdas. But call me that.

I've never actually read the story, but I strongly believe that he and I are quite alike. Did *he* ever go to jail for being jilted in love? I don't know, but I hope he did. The thought provides some comfort. 'Devdas' is still better than all the mouth-breathers calling me Juvenile.

Moreover, he dies at the end. And the way things are going, it doesn't look like my fate is going to be any different.

The Law will kill me. Law—sounds like a Chinese name, doesn't it? But no, I meant the one with the *milord, milord!* Not that the milord-ing would save me. My father's father was a Lord, and trust me, when they finally came for him, he could save no thing and no one. No one because there was no one *to* save. No thing because there were simply too many.

The Law had got him too. Not the milords, mind you, but the Chinese. Not really the Chinese, but the Maoists. He'd died in the makeshift People's Court, set up in the paddy fields he had lorded over, crying, clutching his *dhoti*. I had never seen him or his paddy fields, but I envied the man's death. He died in a place he loved. He got to die someplace that wasn't the Inside.

He died not of a bullet, a sickle or by tripping over his own *dhoti*. As the Court sentenced him to bankruptcy, the capitalist died of heartbreak. Must've been *some* paddy.

You reap what you sow, my father had said when he heard. That was the last time he'd spared his highly erudite words for the late landowner. In that young age, I had foolishly wondered if he hadn't died because he *couldn't* reap what he had sowed.

Paddy causes heartbreak, I learnt that early on. What doesn't?

In one of his private lectures to one of his certifiably over-eighteen female students, my father had lamented the fact that communists just didn't know how to win. He had never specifically said that communists didn't know how to love, but I strongly, strongly believe that we don't.

It wasn't like I had a large pool of communists to test my theory on. The total number of communists whose love lives I knew anything about was two: me and my father. It wouldn't have been proper to go gallivanting amidst the enlightened gentlefolk of Kolkata, asking who they screwed over a cup of communally-grown coffee.

So, given the lack of information, I had no choice but to form an opinion: communism is shitty for your love life. My father was the star of Jadavpur academia, most of his students worshipped him, but the poor man didn't know much love. Not even from those M.Phil girls that stayed over in Father's Night School, wearied from all the education.

And I, Devdas? I didn't have groupies. What I had was a groupie, singular. Her name *wasn't* Paro.

So, what shall I tell you about Paro?

2
THE ARTISAN

Paro

I suppose that's my cue. And I suppose I'm Paro.

A sweet, sharp stinging over the left side of my face—that is my earliest memory of pain and Devdas. There was more to come, from the same source, but I didn't know that yet. I was just six.

'That'll teach you a lesson.' My new Life Coach, a boy my age, his eyes black as Goat, the goat in our house.

As my gaze took in his majestic countenance, I realized that he had complete authority to slap me. There are so many things in the kitchen that you identify based only on where they are placed and what packaging they have. It's much the same with humans. This was a city boy, he was important. The Packaging told me that. That he was older and wiser than his years, his wrinkles told me.

There they were, on the outer edges of his eyes, first convincing me of his absolute righteousness, and as we grew older, of my own corruptibility. That he possessed a superpower only strengthened my belief in this, for he sneezed in exact multiples of six.

'Didn't I tell you to stop cutting it?' he and his Goat eyes demanded an answer, as he wiped the snot from my face with a hankie. 'The grass is alive. They are living beings.'

I looked at the dry *sarkanda* grass in my hand. In my other hand was Mother's sickle, dutifully waiting to cut more *sarkanda* to weave into cheap stools. I hadn't known the grass was alive; that was an interesting titbit.

I yelled something at him, my Haryanvi so thick that the poor boy wouldn't know to distinguish it from a fellow goat's bleating. Tears welled up in my eyes, and I trudged back to the village. At the *chaupal*, the Bengali professor was at it again, raving in his deep-sweet voice. The artisans sat around him, mesmerized.

They said he was teaching us about increased productivity as a collective. So, each day for two hours, everyone took time off from work to listen to him.

Others said that he wanted us to join his Revolution. He promised that other people elsewhere were also Revolutioning somehow. Apparently, the farmers were too content for their own good. It was the time of the handicraftsmen to lead the next set of rabble-rousers.

The productive-collective saw me emerge crying from the woods, the city boy closely following me. His unfortunate father saw us, too. The Old-Goat-boy hit me, I pronounced without being asked.

Mother was in the house, sick, so Father got up and rounded on—what, we're calling him Narayan Mukherjee, right? —Yeah, he rounded on Professor Mukherjee, as did the others.

It didn't occur to me then, but Honour was a big deal in my village, for there was a scarcity of everything else. Men of Haryana either toiled on the fields, or the battlefield. Both were equally noble and life-threatening, though the latter offered the promise of a full meal.

My *muddha*-maker-highway-seller community wasn't involved in either, but Honour they weren't short of. Most of them were on their feet, and in an objective frame of mind, the Professor might have been proud of the way the rabble was roused.

'Accountability above all,' the Professor reassured them when he couldn't placate them. 'Devdas will be punished.'

As they took the scaredy Old-Goat-boy to be locked up with the rest of the chickens, he caught my eye. Between rhythmic sobs, I winked.

Living with seven older brothers and sisters, I had an instinctive awareness of the power of tears. Like all good weapons, the threat of use was more potent than the actual deployment; sometimes, though, you just *needed* to demonstrate.

This particular demonstration would change my life. For the Professor saw the wink. And in his infinite wisdom, he decided that I'd be a great foil for the unruly, motherless child of his. No one else could put him in his place.

How mistaken he was. The wrinkled boy would corrupt me easily, for he was an excellent communicator. He had taught me early on that the best way of getting the message across was an open palm. Not the Buddha kind, but the across-your-face kind. Away from home, from the Honourable people, the occasional open palm *was* my sense of belongingness.

I would come to accept the apathy and the wrinkles and the Goat-eyes.

The Professor spoke to my father. He would take me to Kolkata, where he taught English and Bengali Literature. He would give me an education, the proper kind. How different things would have been, if he'd raised his one kid right, rather than two kids raising each other all wrong.

That was the last of the *sarkanda* I had cut. The grass would always go through many degrees of conversion before it turned into that warm feeling in the pit of my stomach. That blissful absence of hunger.

Grass. *Muddha*. Money. Wheat. Roti.

Don't rinse. Do repeat.

Not anymore. For the next ten years, Bengal beckoned. I didn't know of the epic famines it had borne witness to. For me, Bengal turned out to mean a full stomach. I had the Professor to thank for that.

Checks and Balances, Dev, I'd say to the Goat. There was a power imbalance in the Mukherjee household. Paro was secondary, it was in the Packaging. It'd remain so until I somehow repaid Narayan Mukherjee's debt. And I think I finally have, so much so that some must've spilled over.

I have a much more beautiful name, so why am I still calling myself Paro? Why is Devdas, Devdas?

Well, it all started with that girl. The Saratchandra fan. Chandramukhi.

3
THE COURTESAN

Chandramukhi

The value of every achievement, reward or position is built on the broken dreams of those who never attained it. A thousand schmucks applying for one seat—that's nine hundred and ninety-nine of them making it sweeter for the one person. Simple mathematics.

If *badi didi's* orgasmic 'aahs' and 'oois' are the reward, their value is built on the disappointed dicks of those customers who could never get her there. And she never faked it.

So, if they ask why I fell for Devdas, tell them that he wasn't special. He wasn't the first to my heart, neither did he have a happy dick. The only thing special about him was Paro. Her broken dreams. I know that now.

That's what drew me in, like the zig-zagginess of a snake charmer. In a trance, I slithered into that hand-woven basket with all the other snakes it had consumed.

Before I had been trapped by his countenance, I had been out on a hunt. The alleys of Paharganj had once been like the deep end of the Dal Lake, easy to get lost in, but not anymore. I was sifting through the blind cacophony of enterprise, lost in my search, when I saw him in the flesh for the first time.

Devdas. Such an apt name for him. Beaten. Lovelorn. Chaotic. The maddest in a mad world. The only one who made sense.

His eyes were a hue of hurt, his face bruised, his skin doused red—his own blood or someone else's, I did not know. The Workers gave him a wide berth. He was like a rock, around which they swerved like the mighty Ganga. He was young, no more than seventeen, but he looked like trouble, like the guy who wouldn't have any money afterwards. Like he was already spent.

I recognized him from the photo frame next to the bed I faked most of my orgasms in to keep my own Happy Dick happy. I was seeing him in the flesh for the very first time. In a span of weeks, Devdas had gobbled up a lifetime.

'What—don't!' He recoiled as I touched him. The snake charmer was afraid of snakes. How unfair.

'You look like you need help, mister,' I was firm, like an older sibling. I was, in fact, older. Twenty-one.

He barely saw me, but he registered my grasp on his elbow. 'My friend is upstairs …' He pointed at the narrow, faded-blue staircase that lay hidden behind the creaking double doors; use and old age had broken the marriage between them, and they hardly ever fit together any more.

He called out, almost pleading. 'Chunnilal …' Yeah, that's what we're calling a guy from the twenty-first century.

'Some friend, this Chunnilal. Leaving you here like this.' Still very much the older sibling.

Devdas couldn't conjure up words. I tightened my grip and led the staggering boy through the alleyway, the homeless blood rubbing against my kurti. A couple of Workers threw me warning looks, one smirked. I had caught myself a deadbeat.

He echoed them, whispering in my ear. 'Don't waste your time on me.' Oh, but I *so* wanted to.

Impassively, I walked on. It had been eleven years since my mother and I had walked from Nayi Dilli railway station to this place. Since we had rushed on to a train from Jammu. Since we had left our little village of Sopore under the night's hijab. Since the Uniforms took interest in us. Since Father had blown up a marketplace full of people.

It had felt like the deep end of the Dal, then. That's what Father used to say. Throw the bloody Uniforms in the deep end of the Dal. Throw their laws there. Throw Grandmother's cursed illness there. Inshallah.

The Uniforms would've loved to throw us in the deep end, mother and me. We were traitorous scum, they'd informed us. They'd come knocking, and sure enough, they hadn't believed we knew nothing. Only idiots believe scum, especially Muslim scum. They did something to mother, and next time, they promised to do something more permanent. Terror drove us into the capital for more of the same. Father was comfortable next-door in Tihar, while they debated whether to throw *him* in the Dal. They never stopped debating.

'Who's this?' Our resident Punjaban's eyes were narrow as I set foot inside the haveli, through another set of disjointed double-doors. My foot rested on the discoloured, cheap marble which once upon a time had a geometric pattern that had since been eroded by the dragging feet of countless drunkards. Now the circles bled into the squares.

I had been trying to be inconspicuous, forgetful of the lug of carelessness that hung from my shoulder, and averted the Punjaban's gaze.

'Who's this?' she repeated, pale, fair-skinned, petite, and radiating righteousness. Like many of the others, she thought I was treated special. I was.

I put a finger on my lips, shushing her, and pointed to the temple inside—where the haveli's Goddess was lightly snoring.

'I ought to wake Amma up,' she said, an eyebrow raised.

'As you wish,' I called her bluff, knowing too well she wouldn't dare to.

It wasn't business hours yet. The haveli was chockfull of inactivity. Heaving with angry sensuality. Two hundred years hadn't taught it patience. The walls had been painted over so many times by people of such different tastes that it was difficult to tell where one designer tongue merged into another. Like the earthen cup, the *kulhad*, it was all ready to crumble. We stood at the bottom, and a glance upwards showed nothing but sky. No sign of parched lips. Nobody was drinking yet.

I'd talk to Amma later. Quietly, I led Devdas to my quarters on the roof, up four flights of stairs. Our little building was taller than the rest. My room was taller still. The smell of sweat would never go from this room, but I didn't think he noticed. He was awash in his own stink.

I put Devdas on the creaking diwan-cum-bed, and threw my copy of Saratchandra's *Devdas* over the most essential piece of gear in running a brothel: a first-aid kit. Other than a cupboard, a dozen stacked boxes took much of the space, containing an assortment of less innocent items.

It seemed impossible that he'd ever wake up, so I jumped as sound emanated from his almost still lips.

'You know, sometimes, how the leaves rustle and you think it's raining but it's actually the wind?'

A couple of seconds later, I smiled. 'Yes.'

'I hate that. It's so misleading, that wind. I'd rather have the rain.'

So would I.

Devdas mumbled to someone in a dream. 'Am I mad? I think I am mad.'

I shook my head and realized he couldn't see me. 'No, of course not.' I didn't know if I should go on, so I did. 'Don't worry, even I think that sometimes.'

'Then I shouldn't be asking you. You may be suffering from the same affliction.'

He chuckled. And went to sleep. I went to work dressing his injuries, with the briskness that comes with a lot of practice. The spirit stung his open wound, and his mouth moved to conjure up *her* name.

I knew what had happened to Paro. I knew he had left home afterwards. I knew he was wrecked with grief. I knew his father wanted him back. I knew all of it because I'd been there at the time. In the bed of Professor Happy Dick.

4

MIGRATION

Devdas

Don't believe a word she says. Paro, I mean. She's up to her tricks once again. In the years since my adopted sibling entered my life, I have been extremely civil … except maybe for that one time—or two.

You'll believe her, though. You'll believe anything printed in black Serif across a piece of cheap, reused paper. That's all it takes to make your average Indian feel like a god. Information at his fingertips. Living, breathing, thinking individuals reduced to two-dimensional blots of ink.

'Never believe in the written word,' my father told me once. He didn't know that these very words would come to his rescue years later; good thing he had spoken them.

So, when you read how cruel I was to my adopted sister, I hope you take it with a pinch of salt. Focus on *my* Serif, too. She screwed me, Paro, as much as my own mother.

They weren't wrong about her, you see. My mother, I mean. But then, they never *wrote* anything about her. She was only ever discussed in horny, whispered jokes.

'He showed her channels she'd never seen ...' or 'His connection lasted longer than others ...' or 'She wanted late-night coverage ...' I'd heard them all. I'd even put a few in circulation myself.

Mrs Mukherjee had run off with the local cable guy.

Leaving behind a son who liked to make sex-jokes about her. And a husband who was suddenly a brainy popsicle for sapiosexuals half his age; then there was that glint of nascent misanthropy that made him more attractive. Colleagues whispered in the corridors that Narayan was losing it: their resident intellectual was actually thinking about putting his Marxist theories into practice.

Their fears were well-founded. Weeks later, the remaining Mukherjees packed their bags and left for an expedition across India trying to dig up the remains of the socialist, poverty-absent utopia that India was supposed to have become as soon as the British left. That was Gandhi's idea of freedom, Father said, and it was buried next to his remains. On special days, they hid them both under pretty rangoli patterns made with flowers.

We had gone to dig it out. The only thing us expeditioning Mukherjees returned with, after a year of digging, was a shrill, squeaky, pretty Haryanvi lass.

No angry mobs, no labour unions, no pooling of capital, no Gandhi—just Paro. She was supposed to put a leash on me and she did. Over the years, she did a lot more.

Narayan Mukherjee had truly gone mad, they'd said when the three of us returned, but since this information wasn't in black-on-white, it didn't matter. Nothing they said about him mattered to him until the local newspaper printed it, ten years later, in black-and-white.

BUM-CHIK-CHIK-BUM IN JADAVPUR! Unnamed source leaks private messages between N. Mukherjee and female student (name withheld).

The unnamed source, the story went on to say, had pointed at several past instances of similar behaviour. Since it was in Serif, people believed. After that, they wouldn't let us stay there any longer. The Professor accepted a position in Delhi's eponymous university. The Mukherjees' move to Delhi was a decision that was made for us.

'Never believe in the written word.' Even if it was your own father's dirty text messages printed in the newspaper. I didn't need telling twice.

None of what happened would have happened if my makeshift family hadn't been forced to leave Kolkata. If the paper hadn't gotten hold of that story.

If the unnamed source hadn't been so intent on getting her way. It was that fucking boat-ride.

The *nauka* was gliding through the Hooghly, destroying and birthing the sunset's ripples in the water. It was silent, except for the messy, slurpy sounds from the kissing.

She broke away from my eager mouth for the tenth time that evening. I tried to obstruct her lips again, before she said what I knew she was about to say.

'I feel, Devdas, I feel that I am falling for you,' said the Tuition-Girl. She looked relieved to let it out of her. It had been in her eyes all through the evening—and I was hoping to get done with the good parts before she ruined it.

'Oh, Tuition-Girl, that's wonderful ...' I said with regret, knowing this was the last time I was going to be seeing her. I realized I had been too heavy-handed with John Donne's verses. There were too many sonnets, not enough elegies. No wonder he ended up with twelve children.

However, there was another thing metaphysical poetry was good for. Deflecting questions. The one which was in her eyes required an answer, so I whispered more Donne into her ears, doing my hoarsest voice possible.

No man is an island entire of itself; every man
is a piece of the continent, a part of the main.

I didn't know what she would take away from that, but she took away from it what all people take away from all poetry: exactly what they want to hear.

Tuition-Girl's eyes were wide, thanking her stars at having landed the only sensitive *and* Woke boy she'd ever met. And I was. Sensitive, yes. Woke, hell yes. To gender issues, social stigmas, caste biases, everything minority. The downtrodden needed a voice, and my voice was silky smooth. Especially when I was reciting poetry.

Many had graduated from Father's Night School, but I doubt any had learnt as much as Devdas, the slam poet. The ugly things they buried next to Gandhi were aphrodisiacs. Narayan Mukherjee was a living example. So, I Woke, like him. And I got laid, like him.

The tryst with Tuition-Girl, though, was at an end.

While I was already thinking of ways to dignifiedly, textually break up with Tuition-Girl, I drew her to me for the blissful ignorance of activity. This was one of the few places which gave my dates enough illusion of privacy to make-out. I couldn't take them home—only my father did that. At Prinsep, the boatmen gave you your privacy. Not sure they approved of all the public indecency, but between sleeping hungry and cleaning pre-ejaculates off their boats, I think they preferred the latter—survival is more important to philistines than principles.

The boatman didn't interfere. My adopted little sibling did.

'Are you done yet?'

I came up for air, annoyed.

'The library closes at six,' Paro said pointedly. 'He'll wonder if we're not home by seven.' We were supposed to be studying for our matriculation exams.

I gestured at the boatman to turn the boat around. Paro didn't go back to her place on the other side of the boat. Tuition-Girl and I sat in awkward silence.

I couldn't bear it any more. I turned to Paro.

'Do you have what I gave you earlier?' I asked. It had been her prize for lying.

Paro patted her sling-bag affectionately. 'Right here.'

My hand reached out and Paro blinked. She put the pair of bangles in my hand, wrapped with sepia-coloured plastic.

'Here, for you,' I gave it to my slurpy comrade. Tuition-Girl smiled happily. That was the end to the awkward silence.

I leaned over to Paro and told her I'd buy her another. I leaned back, proud of how well I had handled the situation.

In retrospect, I don't think I had. That's where the trouble started; where Paro decided to expose Narayan Mukherjee, ruin his reputation and force him to accept a teaching position in the capital, where she and I would attend college together away from Tuition-Girl, who I was so clearly in love with.

What can I say? Even Haryanvi lasses with whip-like tongues aren't immune to it. There's just something deeply irresistible about a Woke guy.

5
CHECKS AND BALANCES

Paro

Typical Devdas. Everything's about him. I can't blame him, though. For the larger part of my life, everything *was* about him. That is, until the day I confessed to him, told him what I really felt. It wasn't easy, by any stretch. He was why I had food in my belly, jealousy in my bones, and love in my heart.

I wore his old uniform, slept in the bed he used to wet as a kid, and grabbed at the leftovers of his father's affection. After taking everything that was his, how could I say I wanted him as well? How could *Poor Paro* say it? How could I *not*?

There I was, a pendulum between pride and love. The former kept me from action, while the latter egged me on. Pride won all the time, love needed to win just once. So, I waited, harvesting whatever love I could, storing it in my pockets, guarding it from rodents. Until the day the famine came, and I finally used it. Took some time. Took ten years.

The dichotomy of being treated like a second-class person is that while stubbornly refuting it, you start to believe it. Like I said, there was a power imbalance in the Mukherjee household.

So, whatever part (or whole) I played in defaming the good Professor, I did to negate the imbalance, to take the Bengalis off their home ground, and into neutral territory. Near *my* home.

I knew the Professor was weighing a job in Delhi, but I also knew him well enough to know he wouldn't willingly leave his beloved Bengal. I never had money to travel back to Haryana; it didn't occur to the Professor that I needed to; and I was too proud to ask.

Delhi meant Enterprise. Money. Independence. A chance to be an equal. And finally inform Dev *bhaiya* of the churning inside my dirty, dirty mind.

So, I did what I had to do. Screenshots of the Professor's conversation with his acolytes and a local newspaper was all it took. I had learnt at least one thing from the Bengalis, and it was the power of newspapers. The first one in the continent had been published in Kolkata. *Hicky's Bengal Gazette.* The owner, an Englishman, had accused the

Company's top man in India of suffering from erectile dysfunction. No wonder Bongs loved the news.

Devdas, as usual, sees no one but himself. My actions had almost nothing to do with him. Tuition-Girl, however, was a different story. I don't like people taking my things. And whether or not I said it, that idiot poet *was* mine.

'Okay, Ms Parvati, can you show us what kind of mobile phone you use?'

The silver-haired, sari-clad woman's eyes peered at me over the upper rim of her spectacles. On either side of her sat two portly fellows. Lefty had the part-annoyed, part-complacent smirk of a government employee. Righty was struggling to keep awake.

'I don't have one.'

Righty almost woke up at this. He repositioned his ass, his eyes closed, his mouth surprised.

'Good.' She mistook my penury for choice. 'If anyone really wants to make a call, the Warden's office has a landline.'

I smiled politely, wondering if the interview was over.

'Yes, yes ... we have all the facilities in the hostel.' Her smug, rising eyebrow seemed to be looking for a pedestal to get stuck on.

Lefty glanced at the papers in front of him. 'Says here that you've been admitted to the law college.'

'Yes, sir.'

Righty stirred to life. 'Miss—' He paused, trying to remember my name. He cleared his throat and perused my application form. The rest of us sat unhelpfully and watched him struggle. He gave up.

'So, Miss … can you tell me the name of the main road that leads to the Faculty of Law?'

I paused to assess whether it was a serious question. It was. I shook my head.

Righty hmmm-ed his disapproval. I gauged correctly that they wanted me to look ashamed of myself, so I obliged. Satisfied, the Sari came to the point.

'So, why do you need a hostel? Don't you have your family in the city?'

'No, ma'am, just my guardian. Anyway, I'd like to be closer to the college, so I can concentrate on the—'

Righty interjected, 'What time do you go to sleep?'

By now I knew where this was going. 'Ten-thirty.'

Righty tch-tch-ed. 'Curfew's at eight. Lights off by nine-thirty.'

I smiled compliantly. 'That's good, too. I'll get an early start.'

And that was it. With a curt nod and no words, I was dismissed. I came out of the office, dejected. The next girl went in, her mother breathlessly whispering instructions in her ear until she disappeared behind the door.

My guardian, my victim, appeared in the corridor. Narayan Mukherjee had a laidback stroll. Like he was in no hurry to get from one place to another; like he knew that walking faster or purposefully didn't change the world.

We didn't usually talk much. Like the benevolent government and the lowly citizen, we communicated mostly through application forms and circulars. A couple of days prior, I had placed the hostel form on his table. It told him I needed a couple of hundred rupees for the application fees. It told him I intended to move out of his family-owned CR Park bungalow.

Now, his face was impassive, his eyes staring over my head. 'Congratulations, Parvati. Welcome to Jamia Milia.'

I preferred to get bad news out there as quickly as possible. 'Thank you. I doubt I'll get the hostel, though. The interview was—'

With that same lazy walk, the Professor led me outside. 'You're in. I spoke to a friend in the Faculty.'

'You're sure?'

He nodded, still not meeting my eyes. 'Of course, you can stay at the house whenever you wish to.'

His matter-of-fact generosity put me a little more in his debt. I pinched my arm and promised myself that I'd repay it one day. All of it.

'I can come over on weekends.'

As we walked back towards the rickshaw stand, I stole a glimpse of my new residence. I didn't know it then, but like all things in life, the place would be a battleground. Most of it, I'd have to fight alone. For that first night, though, I'd have someone by my side.

That first night, I met Chandramukhi.

6

LOVE YOU, DEAR

Chandramukhi

The ideal speed to see the world at is ten kilometres per hour. Any slower, you see the ugliness. Any faster, you miss the beauty. How did I arrive at this conclusion? The hard way. I have seen the ugliness and I have missed the beauty. In trying to avoid both, I ran into Paro.

It was past the hostel curfew. I should've been in a hurry to reach the campus, but I was going at my preferred speed. Cold wind caressed my face. I closed my eyes for a bit, feeling the memory of a loving hand on my cheekbone. All I could see through my eyelids was the yellow tint of the streetlights. Easier to process than the neon of Paharganj.

My nights had gotten used to those narrow lanes, the hustle, the Search. There was a little less hiding, a little more truth. In my other life, as a postgraduate in mass communication, all I knew was to be obtuse and vague. Just as well that they were teaching us to communicate.

As I pulled up on the scooter at the hostel entrance, I braced to tuck Chandramukhi away, stick her in my copy of *Devdas* like a bookmark, until the next time she saw neon lights.

The gate was closed. I heard it before I saw it.

'It's barely fifteen minutes past eight!' Paro's voice was ringing with authority even though she didn't have any.

The guard smiled and shrugged, the universal gesture of wilful unhelpfulness.

They noticed me, and it emboldened Paro further.

'There are two of us here now. What are you going to do, turn us away?'

If you ask me, that's exactly what he was going to do. The guard mumbled something. Most words turned into bubbling betel juice in his mouth, but I heard 'my job' in there somewhere. You might hate your job, might be inept at it, or insincere. The prospect of losing it, somehow, is still more unpalatable than the prospect of doing it.

The guard was backing away, he had no reason to help us. Paro sighed, rummaged in her little purse, and came up with a reason. He stopped.

I offered encouragement and moral backing for the bribe, 'Please, *bhaiya*, where will we go at this hour?'

His compassion got the better of him. He grunted and took the money. Before he could unbolt the gate though, the figure of the warden came into view.

'What do you think you're doing?' she barked at him. 'Entry is closed.'

'Ma'am,' Paro began, 'I am sorry, I got a little—'

'Oh yes, isn't it your first day? Already breaking curfew. Tch. Tch.'

Paro seemed to be under the impression that the warden wanted to hear her point of view. She explained to her that she was out buying stuff for her room.

'Whatever the reason, the curfew is for your own safety, girls,' the warden said firmly. 'You girls don't want to be wandering around this time of the night.'

And yet she wouldn't let us in.

'You need to know we can't make exceptions. The gate will open in the morning. You'd do well to consider this a lesson and learn from it.'

She turned and strode inside, satisfied with her contribution towards our long-term personality development. Paro and I stayed motionless, stunned. The guard slinked away before he could be asked to give back the money.

I found my voice.

'You have somewhere to go?'

Paro nodded, then paused, uncertain. 'You?'

'I do.'

Yet neither of us could offer a place to the other. My alternate residence didn't make for suitable small talk, and she couldn't admit that her home wasn't hers to offer me. Hence her hesitancy. Not that I knew it then.

'I can drop you … uh … wherever.'

Her guardian, she said, lived in Chittaranjan Park. It wasn't far, so I offered to drop her. She hopped on the back of my scooter without preamble.

We introduced ourselves. She did not say, 'Thanks. I'm Paro,' and I did not say, 'Chandramukhi. Not a problem.'

I should've been going faster than the ideal speed to view the world, I guess. Maybe then Paro and I would've avoided the sight of two unseemly penises. I had stopped at the traffic signal, basking in the yellow of night-time Delhi.

The boys in the big car next to us fell in love the moment they saw us. They said as much. First, though, they showed they cared.

'You should wear a helmet, dear,' the driver slurred.

I ignored it, while Paro said, 'What?'

'You're flouting traffic rules. A helmet is for your own protection. Maybe we should take you to the cops, dear, so they can tell you.'

Oh, this was all so familiar. The weight in the pit of my stomach momentarily pinned me to the spot.

One of the guys on the backseat chuckled. 'Maybe she doesn't like to use protection. Do you, beautiful?'

With practiced hands, the two in the backseat instantly had their penises out for our viewing pleasure. The deftness would be something to envy even for a skilled magician pulling a rabbit out of a hat.

I revved the pitiful engine of my electric scooter, trying not to panic, keeping the speed over the ideal ten, but not enough to seem like we were running. I knew they liked us running.

'Motherfuckers.' Paro's voice had no fear, no uncertainty. Just anger.

They caught up in a few seconds. 'Hey, you just jumped a signal. We'll have to take you in.'

I gave up the pretence. We *were* running, and I *was* scared. There was no running from *that* fact. I sped up as much as I could.

I didn't see them, but I could hear them. Which, funnily enough, was worse.

'Love you, dear!'

Tske chhuk myon jigur. That's what my mother used to say. It comes easy to mothers and molesters, I suppose, saying they love you.

I never told my mother I loved her. It seemed harder, somehow, in my native language. Too intimate, too corny. That hadn't been the case with the men I'd been with—the fact that I didn't have to say it in Kashmiri probably helped. As did the fact that I was lying.

The boys in the car had started singing songs. I noticed one of them had a college-hoodie on. I wondered if they were out at night because his hostel had a curfew too.

Somehow, instinctively, I had brought us in front of the local *thana.* The boys stopped a hundred metres off, expectant, waiting for us to go inside the compound. We did.

After a few moments of stunned silence, Paro began to get off. My heart sank. Was she naïve enough to actually go to the cops?

She gauged my expression and told me she just needed to feel the ground beneath her feet; she had no intention of being interrogated for a second time in as many days. I didn't ask what she meant by that.

'I think we should leave,' I prodded. A couple of *beedi*-smoking constables were looking our way.

Paro checked to see if the car had left, and got on, muttering, 'If only those fuckers didn't have your number plate, I *would* have lodged a complaint ...'

It hit me that Paro wasn't naïve at all, and probably a bit braver than myself. It was this righteous anger, the inability to take things lying down, which would alter the course of our lives, and spark a revolt in the coming days that'd put those Marxists to shame.

It would also make Paro realize the power of an idea; whether that was a good thing or bad, I couldn't decide.

We drove the rest of the way in silence, except for some directions on Paro's part. When she asked me to stop outside a red-brick house, my breath got stuck halfway up my throat. I had been here before. I *knew* the middle-aged man who came to the gate, groggy from his nightly drink.

'Professor,' I blurted out.

Narayan Mukherjee strained his eyes to see who it was.

'You know each other?' asked Paro.

The Professor smiled. 'Yes, we met during one of my lectures here in Delhi.'

I nodded with vigour for this much was not a lie.

'You really helped me, Professor.' Another non-lie. 'I never got to thank you enough.'

He gulped, for that was a lie. I had thanked him many, many times over. He cleared his throat.

'If I'm not wrong, you are a mass communications student now? Postgraduation in Jamia?'

I nodded. Paro used the happy coincidence to evade the question of why she was here instead of the hostel. She thanked me and went inside. The Professor gave me an almost imperceptible nod as he bolted the gate. And then he went inside the house that I knew every inch of.

Tske chhuk myon jigur.

Narayan Mukherjee was one of the many men to have said that they loved me. He was the only one I somewhat believed.

After all, he was a patron.

7
PROTEST

Devdas

I have a theory. Greatness comes from never looking down. Literally, I mean. All the great, distinguished men of history, I doubt a single one has seen his feet. Most of the hoi polloi spend their lives looking down, at the phone, at the alphabet, at themselves. So much so that when they finally look up, it's not enlightenment they experience, but a dull, muscular pain in the back of their necks.

Try it. Look upwards for a minute. Feel that dull ache? Most people aren't bothered by it. A few are. A few have terrible foot hygiene.

Like that badass girl from Jamia, the one who'd been barred out of her own hostel in the middle of the night. The one who'd sent an anonymous letter to the Vice Chancellor and the National Commission for Women. The one who'd lit the match that would consume the Man's cages.

I bet little Paro couldn't describe her feet if one asked her to.

Her small act of looking upwards had been enough to drive We the Feminists into a frenzy. Within a few months, the wildfire had reached the University of Delhi. Curiously enough, it seemed that nowhere did women want to be told what to wear, where to go, and whom to fuck. Of course, I was vehemently with them, especially on that last part.

So, I stood in the Arts Faculty, under the shadow of an indifferent Swami's statue. Around fifty of my English Lit comrades stood around me, holding placards ranging from 'No Chains. Can't lock us up' to 'No Chains. Lest we be Kinky.' The frenzied optimism reminded me of home.

'*Pinjra Tod!*' I yelled from the raised platform.

'Break the patriarchy!'

'*Pinjra Tod!*'

'Break the patriarchy!'

That went on for a bit.

It hadn't taken me long to regain my status as the Woke boy in this new place. An open mic of slam poetry was all it took. Now everyone knew how I missed my lovely whore mother. I was fucked up enough to be blindly followed without feeling bad about oneself.

And follow me they did. Our screaming march through the campus arrested many eyeballs and prickled a few eardrums. Those were the milder injuries destined to happen that day.

Then came the saffron flags. Right-wingers have a habit of making everything about the Indian Culture. They might not be able to define what it is, but they are very certain about things that are not it. Women demanding autonomy over their own bodies felt, well, not it. I took a few bold, brave steps towards them.

That is, until I realized that the flags were attached to sticks, which were thick, which aborted protests, and—once I had the opportunity to experience it first-hand—left huge red welts when ungently applied to the skin. At that point in my life, before I did to Paro what I did to Paro, pain was a novel concept. Best observed from afar.

Since I was the one yelling the loudest, the Flagbearers gravitated towards me. It hadn't helped that I had taken those few bold, foolish, welcoming steps towards them. The most active of the activists, a short, stout fellow, yelled to the heavens the name of his favourite Hindu deity, probably asking for strength to do what he was going to do.

There was a huge SMACK! and I was on the ground, holding my ass, which screamed in protest. My comrades did the same. As I lay on the ground, I finally believed in God. For he did hear his stout follower, he *had* given him strength. That's what the pain felt like. Divine intervention.

There was another SMACK! followed by a CLICK. Someone appreciative of my condition felt it best to capture it for posterity. Someone who knew it would be worth something.

You know those newspaper photos? On roadwalks, on the back of buses, on flyers, in the wrapping of your *jhal muri*? The ones that stir your soul, inspire you, enrage you? The ones that look like the Government's Fault?

That was me, getting my ass kicked. The hunger-strikers of the Jan Lokpal movement didn't hold a candle to me; I looked emaciated as fuck. And sure enough, a couple of English dailies carried it the following day.

I couldn't hog all the credit, though. The still frame that made me a quasi-celebrity also encased my tormentor. He was a splash of saffron in the background, a vertical stripe of vermillion on his forehead, raised stick, yelling to the heavens.

Say what you must, the guy was passionate. It was a frenzied, unlimited passion I had seen before. In my father. It hadn't lasted the Bitch's Betrayal, or our unfruitful travels, but when it was there, I could have sworn it was infinite.

Now, I didn't know anything about this guy, only that he had my father's naïve passion. I didn't plan to see him again, nor stick around long enough to get to know him in case I did. Yet, the best laid plans tend to go kaput. My father knew this by now, as did the Jan Lokpal hunger-strikers.

To know this for myself, I would have to run into that guy again. My mentor, my tormentor.

Where would I be now, if not for my dear, addled friend Chunnilal?

Yes, we *are* calling him that.

It was a pride parade. This time, too, he was a Flagbearer. Not saffron, though, but all the colours of the rainbow.

The proud had gathered right in the centre of Connaught Place. In the underground marketplace beneath our feet, the hawkers of Palika Bazaar proudly sold counterfeit apparel, counterfeit electronics, and A-grade genuine porn for all sexual preferences.

Chunnilal was engaged in an argument with a sparkly young man dressed in drag. A willowy gown, a weird hairdo, and the works. Chunnilal, standing closer to me, was almost unrecognizable. The *tika* was gone, as was the crazed look in his eyes. There were violet highlights in *his* weird hairdo.

'—I *don't* have an opinion about it one way or the other, my love,' the Drag Queen was flailing her arms about dramatically, 'no government has cared about us, so why should we care about them? I am apolitical, darling, and I don't give a flying fuck—'

Chunnilal interrupted her—wait, it *is* 'her', right? I get confused by these gender-specified pronouns. Facebook gives you seventy-one gender options. Maybe I could do mnemonic slam poetry on it. We the Woke should keep up. Till then, if it looks like a woman, talks like a woman, maybe I should call it 'her'?

'Apolitical? *Apolitical?* What—how could you—?' For a few moments, Chunni ran out of words. His face was red again, the crazed fervour was back, and he started rummaging in his pockets.

The lady might've been apolitical, but she wasn't a total idiot. She had the sense to take a couple of steps back. Chunnilal took out a phone from his pocket and covered that distance within half a second as he shoved it in her face.

'See?' he said triumphantly. Before she could get a good look at the phone, Chunnilal turned it towards his own eyes and began reading loudly. '"The worst illiterate is the political illiterate, he doesn't hear, doesn't speak, nor participates in the political events."'

The Drag Queen was beating a retreat now, and Chunnilal was following her, and I was following him. All three of us were bumping into people, but only Chunnilal's shambling progress was accompanied by a Google-enabled ideological rant.

'"The political illiterate is *so* stupid that he is proud and swells his chest saying that he hates politics,"' Chunnilal called after her as she disappeared into the crowd. He was sufficiently pleased with his victory, until he saw me.

He frowned, trying to place me. When he did, all he could enunciate was an 'oh'.

'You're quoting a damn Marxist playwright?' I exclaimed. 'What kind of a pseudo-conservative are you?'

He shrugged unapologetically. 'The fake kind?'

I wanted to scream and knock the living daylights out of him. I didn't, since the memory of our last meeting was still seared into my left buttock.

'I am a blogger, see? I write about the perspective of today's youth on issues that concern them. The youth is varied in its sexual preferences. Just like the youth is conservative.'

'So, what? You go around in these rallies pretending to be one of them? For your blog?'

He shrugged. 'I was pretending *then*. I am not pretending right now, if that helps.'

'So, you mean—you are—I mean, are you—?'

'Queer?' he grinned. 'Aren't we all somewhat?'

I nodded, pretending to be in agreement, unsure about what I was agreeing to.

'What if those lunatics found you out? Isn't it dangerous?'

'Isn't everything?'

I learned that he had the skill of answering questions with questions. He instantly got my grudging respect. Not least because he reminded me of a young Narayan Mukherjee. Back when the Professor would take up a lost cause. Back when he *did it* and not just *said so*. Back when he could inspire me. Back when *he* had my grudging respect.

He smiled sagely. 'It's for their education,' he said, pointing to the universe in general. We agreed on that much, I suppose. The universe needed educating. 'So, the beating you took ... was, well, for the greater good.'

I can't say that made me feel better. He extended his hand, not introducing himself as Chunnilal.

I paused before taking it, never saying Devdas.

Our brief bromance was broken by an altercation happening towards the edge of the gathering. As we went closer to take a look, it seemed that some passers-by had passed some less-than-appreciative comments towards a transwoman. Her friend was giving it back to them.

It was a teachable moment, and like a good educator, my pulse quickened. I moved forwards, while Chunni came to a full stop. I gestured for him to follow and back me up.

'Wait ...' he was staring at the muscled men who'd started the commotion. 'I know that guy.'

That didn't make me stop. What made me stop were the fists with worn-out knuckles, threatening, imminent. They instantly made me rethink some life choices. Getting beaten up once had been martyrdom, getting beaten twice would just be bad judgement. It was unbecoming of gentlefolk. I was supposed to champion the plebs, not join their ranks.

'Let's bounce, man,' I muttered. He didn't move, and a few moments later, I registered what he'd said. 'Wait, what? You *know* him? From where?'

'He was a part of the counter-protesters ... that day ... the day we met. He was the one who organized us, gave us weapons.'

I frowned. So that's two peaceful demonstrations this guy was responsible for disturbing. 'This isn't a coincidence.'

Chunni nodded, a sudden gleam in his eyes. 'I smell a story, Dev.'

I noticed Chunni's eyes reflect sudden fear. Before I could do anything but turn to look, the beast of a man Chunni had recognized was pointing a gun at the transwoman's friend. That's when I heard it. The Big Bada Boom.

I ducked pre-emptively, as did a few others who were quick on their feet. The rest saw the shot being fired. It was like a bomb going off—both in its occurrence and consequence. There was an immediate stampede.

By the time we gathered ourselves, a young man our age lay at the edge of the park, his brains splattered all over the grass, his prostrate figure shielded by the shadow of an indifferent, mammoth Indian flag that fluttered in absolute silence over us.

8

HONOUR

Paro

I didn't expect to lose the ability to make friends, even perfunctory ones. I guess nobody really does. It happens gradually, so you don't notice it. And before you know, old friends have moved on, and new ones are nowhere to be found. Even after you've been eve-teased together …

I saw Chandramukhi a couple of times in the campus after that night, but all I got was a brisk hello. She avoided me like the plague, and I couldn't understand why. My newest friend had better things to do, I suppose.

As did my oldest friend. Even though I visited the house as often as I could, Dev was too busy to spare his attention for old Paro. After the shootout at Connaught Place, he just sort of disappeared. I mean I could still see him and stuff, but he wasn't really there.

It was that Chunnilal. Of course, *he* had no trouble making new friends. And now they were up to something. Which didn't include me.

Good or bad, he had always been there. Now he wasn't.

Was I already in love with him by this point? I honestly don't know. My love for Dev didn't have a *when*. It didn't happen at a time, or a place, or a moment or a word. It happened *to* me much like life. Constantly. Inevitably. He was the cigarette smoke corroding my very being. I knew it would kill me, but in this moment, the smoke was the air that I breathed in and out. How does one stop breathing?

I don't know what I had expected when we moved to Delhi. That out of the house they had let me into, I would feel less indebted to the Mukherjees? That out of his element, Dev would find comfort in me? Or that chucked out of Kolkata, my adopted brother and father would be more like me—outsiders?

I am not sure. I just expected something to change. It didn't, really. Narayan and Dev Mukherjee were embraced by the city like long-lost brothers. Even though they started from scratch—or wherever it is that people with privilege start from. And I was still an outsider, lurking on the edges, unsure of my place.

Since it seemed I was destined to remain on those edges, I concluded that it might be prudent to familiarize myself with them. Towards the end of September, I found myself on the outskirts of Delhi, in a Haryana state roadways bus. I was headed to the one place that had been home before I had a concept of one.

By the time I learnt what home meant, it came with the acute knowledge of not being in it.

My recollections of Haryana were a slow-cooked stew of colours and sensations, too mild to be classified as memories. Going back, I didn't remember enough about the place to have any expectations from it. This place had spit me out once, and I'd be a fool to expect anything else.

The village was no longer a village, and not yet a town. It seemed stuck somewhere between civilization and lawlessness. The houses were big, though merely functional. There was as much space for the livestock as there was for people. There were doors, and all of them were open. There were roofs and walls, but the elders sat outside. Somehow, without coherent sentences, the news of my arrival reached my former home before I did.

My mother looked through her *ghunghat* at me, for all intents and purposes, a stranger. She greeted me in a language I no longer understood. I folded my hands and she approved.

My father was old and worn out, nervous and unsure in my presence. I was important, my Packaging told him that. He smiled sweetly at me, deferential. It wasn't like I had any expectations, but it's funny how you can still be surprised.

From what I understood, three of my six siblings were still alive. Including me, that was four out of seven. That's a decent ratio, apparently, since my mother was somewhat proud when she said it.

As we sat inside the brick house, loud voices and footsteps forebode the arrival of two men. One of them was a cocky constable, his face a never-ending, self-assured smirk. It was hard to say if his swagger had contributed to him getting the uniform, or the other way around. The one leading him in was a towering young man. Besides his beastly physique, he carried an air of authority greater than that of the policeman.

The uninvited visitors nodded at my father, who got up from his place and bent low before the two, yelping at my instantly veiled mother to get tea. Just about to take seats on a *chaarpai*, the men spotted me, stopping mid-bow, their backsides hanging precariously over their seats.

The constable scowled at me suspiciously, his body-language hostile. He hurled a series of expletives at my father in thick, angry Haryanvi. I also caught the words *Dilli-waale* and *newspaper-waale,* as he pointed at me.

Father was terrified, tongue-tied. It was mother who got a quick word in. The word was *beti.* Daughter. The constable stared at me closely, and his face softened in wonder.

'Paro? The Professor's Paro?' He might very well have discovered signs of extra-terrestrial life. There were signs of recognition on the young man's face, too. He'd heard of the alien as well.

The constable smiled sheepishly. His companion strode forwards and extended a hand. I shook it.

'I've heard about you. Myself Bhuvan Chaudhary. You've come from Kolkata?'

'Delhi. I am studying law in Jamia.'

Bhuvan raised an eyebrow, impressed. The constable began to fidget. They were here for a reason. I offered them their privacy, and they accepted it without a word. I wandered outside on to the street. I could feel Bhuvan's eyes on me.

All across the paved street, men, women and children sat with a bunch of nylon rope and rubber tyres. The sweet old *sarkanda* grass had grown obsolete. Spat out unceremoniously.

I sat down on a finished *muddha* next to a skinny teenage boy who was working on its twin.

'You're from Dilli?' he asked me, his eyes sparkling, his hands moving with dexterity, giving shape to the *muddha* with the nylon rope. 'You're here about the slut?'

'I am sorry, what did you just say?'

'The slut they buried last night.'

He got my attention. I feigned knowledge, and that's how I gained it. The boy recounted the story with relish. The woman had eloped with a Dalit man last week. There was chaos, allegations thrown around. Then the woman's family called her back, told her they forgave her. She came back, hopeful. That was last night.

The boy was excited, he felt he was a part of something bigger. Something had Happened, and he knew.

'So, that's why the constable is going house to house, asking questions? He's trying to get the truth?' I murmured to myself.

The boy gave me a funny look. Almost pitiful. 'He's a Brahmin.'

'So?'

He tut-tutted. 'He knows the truth. He needs to go to one house only. One family only.'

A moment of confusion, then chills down my spine. *The girl's family.* My family.

I understood the constable's presence now. And his alarm at seeing me—an outsider. The deed was done. Bhuvan and the constable were here to make sure the family didn't grow a conscience. It was a social contract between caste-brothers. No complaint, no case.

I turned to look at the house, and the silhouette of my father through the window. Was he there when they killed her? Was he smiling that innocent smile? I knew then what I had only suspected before. These people *were* strangers.

The men exited from the house. They seemed more relaxed. Brotherly.

'Will we be seeing you more often?' Bhuvan asked me as he went past. The teenage boy deferentially took his work elsewhere.

'I'm not sure.'

'We could do with more educated, enthusiastic young people around the community. There's a whole world out there we aren't a part of.' He pointed at the street full of *muddha*-makers. 'You're from here, you can bridge that gap. Think about it.'

I kept watching him as he walked away with the constable, until I realized what I was doing. About to go back inside, a thought came to me, and I stopped by the teenage artisan.

'What happened to the boy she ran away with?'

'Nothing. He's back home, in *their* side of the village.'

'How come?'

'He had a family. And those people make police complaints these days.'

I had been in Jamia's Law School for a few months, but this was my most important lesson about the justice system yet. What would fetch more per square inch of Honour, killing the Dalit boy, or their own caste-traitor girl? They had wanted the former, but had settled for the latter.

Because Honour felt better outside jail.

9

THE SEARCH

Chandramukhi

They say you can smell the *ittar* in the open drains of Kannauj. Flowing from the perfume factories, mixed with the workers' sweat. You could almost taste hope on the tip of your tongue. I didn't know if it was true, but I imagined it to be blissful.

As I spent my nights walking through the streets of Paharganj, Searching, I often wondered what it smelled like here. Sex? Desire? Wrongdoing? I couldn't put my finger on it. My other senses were just so overwhelmed.

'AZAADI!'

The valley I was born in was much more tranquil. Except for the time when it wasn't. The chaos took everything and everyone. And left me all—

I got it. The smell. I know what it was. It dripped from the core of my being, just as it streamed through the streets of Paharganj.

Loneliness.

The place thrived not on lust, or love, but loneliness. It didn't matter that you couldn't walk without bumping into someone. You didn't bump into a person, but into a crowd. Like most of civilization this was a marketplace. Transactional in nature. Not one real human connection.

Maybe that's why I was so desperate to meet my father.

'AZAADI!'

It wasn't as if I didn't know where he was, but there were over ten thousand inmates in Tihar. I just didn't know *who* he was. No name, no knowledge as to exactly why he was on the Inside. The last time I saw him was in the Valley, unable to grasp that I might never again see either. How could a child, one who didn't understand the concept of forever, begin to understand the enormity of never?

The time when I could force my mother to tell me was long gone. Luckily, though, there were still people on the mainland who cared about what went on in the Heaven on Earth. I knew of one. An Angel of the Valley. An activist-politician. A bona fide Comrade.

'AZAADI!'

I looked through my mask. Night had fallen. The JNU campus was revelling and revolting at the same time. The man that led the sloganeering was wearing a mask, but I knew who he was. I had been tracking him for quite some time.

Comrade Angel raised another battle-cry from the parapet. And the students below responded. As did I.

'AZAADI!'

'AZAADI!'

I did not want *azaadi.* It was a childish notion, and I wasn't a child any more. No one is ever really free. No, all I wanted was to have a word with the Comrade before he disappeared like he usually did. Already I could see the Uniforms filming the event.

The cover of the night gave me anonymity, but I still tied the mask tighter around my face. I seeped like blood through a wound deeper into the crowd, getting closer to the man who could help me find my father.

Suddenly, the crowd began collapsing in on itself, the wound closing. Another bunch of placard-holders and slogan-shouters were seemingly intent on occupying the space we stood on. Drowning our voices with theirs. Right-wingers.

'Goli maaro saalon ko!' Kill the fuckers. The fuckers being us.

One of the men calling for my death was dear old Devdas. Of course, I didn't know it then. I didn't know him then. Except as a photograph on his father's bedside.

As the slogans and anti-slogans raised in tempo, I saw the Comrade Angel slip out from the back. I followed him, terrified that I was going to lose him again. He entered a building, found an isolated maintenance room, and removed his mask.

'Comrade!' I hissed as he jumped, eyes darting around, as terrified at having been found as I was at the prospect of losing him.

'Comrade …' he breathed a sigh of relief. The mask over my own face reassured him.

'I'm so glad I ran into you today …' I removed the physical mask and wore my usual one. He was just another patron, that's all. In a world full of Men, just one more Unhappy Dick.

'Do I know you, Comrade—?' he muttered.

'Chandramukhi.' I stepped closer, conspiratorially. 'Actually, I need your help. It's about my father. I know it's not a good time to—'

His eyes lit up. 'Tell me.'

I told him everything I had to go on, which wasn't much. My mother's name. The year of my father's incarceration. Our move to Delhi. Mother's Choice.

He grew angrier with each word. Some people are like that, who get angry or sad on behalf of others. The Angel was one of them. 'I cannot imagine what you must've done to survive, my girl. Rest assured, I'll find where they are keeping your father. This is what we're fighting against, you know? And I am glad you joined the fight.'

Comrade Angel didn't need to know the truth, so I just nodded. I didn't want to fight. I just wanted to survive. Preferably, not by myself.

When they had taken my father away, it had seemed all so inexplicable. Why would a man give up the comfort of his home, the love of his family, the beauty of his village, and go kill a bunch of people? I blamed him, like they did, for everything was his fault. I never imagined that one day they'd be saying the same about me.

In the weeks that followed my encounter with the Angel of the Valley, I saw my masked face printed on newspapers and flickering on TV channels. Everyone wondered about the anti-nationals of JNU. Why were these anti-nationals anti-national? Wasn't the benevolence of a loving country enough?

In my class at Jamia, it was all anyone could talk about, conjecturing, trying to explain the inexplicable. Any moment now, and I'd be found out ... but then, I was no stranger to that feeling. I already led a double life. Back in Paharganj, none of the Workers had an extra fuck left to give about matters of treason.

In the din of debates and the overtness of opinion pieces, no one speculated that one of the traitors was just a girl looking for her father. People simply argued with Echoes of whichever truth they believed in. I was relieved; had the reaction been measured and rational, they may have caught Comrade Angel before he could do what he'd promised.

They would move on, I knew. The everyday voter forgets things easily. That's the only way to survive, to not remember how things were. So that you can't compare them to how things are. That's how you stay sane and stupid and sure of yourself.

In the interim, though, both sides needed to show they were pissed off and would remain so for the foreseeable future. So, there were hunger strikes and work strikes. And since the purpose of these strikes is to prevent *other* people from working, I got my patron saint all to myself one warm afternoon, his classes suspended for the week.

'I found my father.'

I didn't look at the Professor when I told him this. He wouldn't be angry; he rarely ever was. For some reason, I was afraid he'd be hurt.

'You did,' he noted, putting his clothes back on. I stared resolutely at his study table. At a monochrome photograph of a young, boorish kid smirking at me. Little Devdas.

'I know he's in jail, but I have to see him,' I muttered, 'you can understand.' I knew his relationship with Devdas was taut as a tightrope. 'You have a son. You'd go to see him.'

Narayan Mukherjee sighed. 'Why would my son ever be in jail? Anyway, you're no longer a child, Chandramukhi. You don't need my approval.'

I finally faced him, in his half-askew *kurta-pajama*, almost comical.

'I do need your advice.'

'I advised you to leave Paharganj for good. You are still there.'

Sometimes I hated how dispassionately logical he was.

'Well, if your advice is contingent on my following it, maybe you should keep it.'

He sighed, and softened. 'You know I don't object to the business they conduct in that place. I am not a prude, nor am I ignorant of historical context. The modern red-light districts are nothing but a by-product of the brothels the British *constitutionally* maintained for their soldiers. My concern is not morality or legality, but your well-being.'

I believed him. It didn't change anything.

'And I have told you I cannot leave. Not yet, anyway.'

He assessed me, and then moved on. 'About your father—'

'I need to meet him.'

'You believe he'll be the answer to the question that plagues you.'

'Or that he can point me to it. He's the only one who can—'

'Do the impossible?' he clicked his tongue. 'Never make people your heroes. They are indefensible. And Gods? They don't exist.' He sat beside me, looked at me with those old, weary eyes. 'I learnt it the hard way. You must never believe in a man. They can tear a man down. But a way of thinking, an idea? That's immortal.'

'What has that got to do with—?'

'Because he's just a man, your father. He cannot defend himself against what's been thrown at him. And you'd be a fool to expect anything more.'

'I don't expect him to be perfect. I expect him—well—I—I don't expect anything, to be honest.'

'Expect him to be a father. No more, no less. Also know that he believes in something fanatically. Jailed men often do. That's usually the reason they are there in the first place.'

'You believe in things. How come you're not in jail?'

'Maybe I am not as brave as your father.' He felt slighted, and I knew he was going to be abrasive now. 'Or maybe I cared for my family more than he did for his.'

That stung. I got up and got dressed. The Professor kept his eyes on me. As I made to leave, he drew up the sleeve of his *kurta* and pointed at an oblong scar on his arm.

'You know, I think this is one of the noblest things we've done for our children.' He ran a finger over the scar. 'The vaccine for smallpox. I remember it stinging like a bitch. It carried the risk of severe side-effects, but an entire generation of people went through it. They took the pain, the fear, the uncertainty. And spared their children. That's what a parent is supposed to do—pass on the best of us and keep the rest.' He took a step closer. I had never seen him this earnest.

'When you meet him, remember to take from your father his best bits. His strength. His ability to believe. Don't take *what* he believes in. Those fears aren't meant for you.'

'I have kept your bad bits at bay, Professor. What makes you think I won't do the same with him? You know I am not that easy.'

The Professor smiled, betraying a rare fondness. 'I know. And I also know why you really wish to see him. It's why I was drawn to you, that first time we met.'

I raised an eyebrow. 'Why *were* you drawn to me?'

He busied himself in making the bed, his back to me so I couldn't see his face.

'I was lonely.'

10

THE FIGHT CLUB

Devdas

The murder of the Ambedkar University student at the pride parade was breaking news for a while. The people had found their new messiah: a twenty-year-old kid who wanted to change the world. Of course, like most messiahs, he was luckily not around to see the circus being played out in his name.

Apparently, he was gay. Which was unhelpful, to say the least. Gay people don't exist in this country, and those that don't exist, can't vote. And were you fortunate enough to sight one, you couldn't scare them of what-would-happen if so-and-so came to power. They were screwed regardless of who was in power.

But Dalits, well, *they* exist. In fact, they were discovered in the fifties. And they vote. Thus, politicians can fight for them. So that's who he was, a Dalit Kid who died fighting the Brahmanical forces. He was the new rallying cry in campuses. They moved on from *Pinjra Tod*. There was a new kid on the block. And he wanted Justice.

For once, though, I was on the other side of Justice. Along with Chunni, I was undercover. He had recognized the rioters at the parade. He had seen them hidden amidst with far-Right student protesters. They seemed to be in their mid-thirties; they weren't students, and if they were, then they must have been really bad ones.

In the days after the Dalit Kid had stopped a bullet with his head, Chunni was on a mission to track down the men that did it. Not to turn them in, obviously, but for his blog.

Of course, he needed my help. Of course, I was glad to offer it, to atone for my feudal heritage. Of course, it wouldn't end well for me. Even if I'd known, I don't think it would have made much of a difference. He was my spirit animal. Truer than me. Wilder than me. A constant reminder.

He found the men he was looking for, and soon, we found ourselves at an *akhada* in Paharganj. Desi bodybuilders training in a hundred-year-old *haveli.* Oiled and lubed and ready for action. Glistening in the sunlight. The weights went up and down. The air was violated with sounds of indecent huffing and puffing and grunting. Two men grappled in the centre of the atrium, making violent love.

I gulped with a dry throat, while Chunni pressed me on. I hesitated, though I knew what I was here for. It wasn't like I was having second thoughts. I had already had them. In fact, I was on the third or fourth serving. I cursed the moment I had agreed to come.

'They are *pehelwaans,*' Chunni had informed me. 'From Old Delhi. Given patronage by a certain political party. Paid to break up protests, or taint them with violence.'

'And you got in?' I had asked, with enthusiasm. It would be short-lived.

'Well, yes, they think I am like them,' Chunni seemed shifty, 'I have a pretty solid cover. But—'

I waited. My enthusiasm was at its peak. It could only go down from there.

'—I had to tell them about you. An upper-caste Hindu boy who'd been seduced by the communists. And … uh … you saw how misguided you were. You're here to do your penance.'

That was when the enthusiasm died. 'I thought we were undercover!'

'I couldn't risk them recognizing you from the newspaper photo. So, I—I pre-empted it. A good lie must have a bit of truth in it.'

That's when I had agreed to come. And now we were in the lion's den.

There was a sudden eclipse. I felt it was happening inside my head, until I saw a beast of a man blocking the sun. The last time I had seen him, he held a smoking gun in his hand …

'This is the Brahmin boy?' the Hulk asked. Chunni nodded.

I had never lifted weights before, but as the Hulk's hand came to rest over my left shoulder, I knew what it felt like. The chunky, oily fingers moved aside my collar and found their way inside my shirt, rummaging painfully around my collarbone.

'Where is your *janeu*, lad?' he growled at me.

'My what?'

'*Janeu.* Your sacred thread. You're a Brahmin, are you not?'

I put my head down, remembering the time we burnt the Manusmriti on campus in Kolkata. I remembered the vigorous nodding along with my peers' 'all-savarna-men-are-pigs' assertions.

It was sacrilege in my old world to accept it; it would be suicide in this world not to. Chunni gave me a nudge.

'Yes, my grandfather was—I mean, yes, I am.'

A moment of silence as the Hulk judged me. Then, a gentler, kinder note. 'It's all right. You've been influenced by those fucking Naxalites. You'll no longer be working for the enemy. You'll be with your own people here.'

In one melodramatic sweep, he lifted up his *kurta*, to reveal, apart from the nicely-toned abs, his own *janeu*.

'It's signifies your second birth. In a way, it's good you didn't wear it till now. You haven't been reborn yet.' He slapped my shoulder. 'Today, you will be.'

Before I knew it, Chunni and I were being pushed into the muddy atrium, as everyone gathered around to watch the new meat.

'Have you ever lived a day without fear?' he taunted from the side-lines.

Not today, I was sure. Being stuck in this den of bloodthirsty man-children, I couldn't think straight. Had I been able to, I would've known the answer to his question was a definite no.

'God and Nature have made us fearful beings, for our own survival.' He began walking towards us. 'But we are not meant to be so. We are meant to rise above.'

Chunni was listening with rapt attention, nodding his head, playing the part of the blind zealot.

'Pain. It's what Man fears above all else. Beyond reason, beyond expectation. Physical, psychological, spiritual pain. The fear of physical pain is the first to enter us, so it must be the first to leave.'

Before I could marvel at the clarity of thought of this particular brute, he was upon us, pulling me and Chunni within a foot of each other, growling in our ears.

'Watch, now.' He made a gesture and instantly, two grown men in their prominently-tight-undies descended on to the mud. 'TEN!'

The men went berserk. BAM. Their lubricated bodies slammed against each other with the force of a small bomb. I felt the concussion wave from ten feet away. I barely even noticed the Hulk count down from ten. Nine. Eight. Seven.

If I didn't know better, I would say the men were trying to kill each other. I had read the Greek epics. I was aware of the term, murderous rage. I only understood it now. No elegance. Just brutal destruction. Six. Five. Four.

No fear. I understood what the Hulk meant. These men were unafraid. They didn't care how much damage they took. They didn't care how much damage they did. Thrashing in the mud. Panting. Huffing. Puffing. Three. Two. One.

The Hulk threw dry mud at their eyes. And they broke apart, as though coming out of a trance. Each iota of strength and willpower drained from them. They hunkered on out of the ring.

The Hulk turned to us. 'You have ten seconds. No rules. No restrictions. You don't have to be beautiful. You don't have to have grace.'

Chunni looked determined. He took an aggressive stance. Ready to do it, and not just say so.

I took a step back. 'Wait—I am not ready—'

'TEN!'

I don't particularly remember the details of the next ten seconds. I erased them from my mind. Or maybe my mind has erased them for me. Suffice to say, my first time was quite forgettable.

Chunni told me later that we did well. He need not have; the bruises on my torso were indicators enough. We were officially part of the Fight Club. For-hire musclemen. We would be called upon whenever our services were needed. Standing behind leaders at a speech. Standing in the crowd in a moving rally. Protesting. Turning a protest into a mob. Rioting. Whatever the patrons asked.

We were just bodies. Two more bodies, in the sea of opinion. We were called upon earlier than I expected, though. The first assignment was a seditious, separatist event planned at JNU. One we needed to stop.

I screamed for the deaths of the masked anti-nationals as loudly as I could. Not knowing Chandramukhi was one of them. Not knowing her fate was tied to mine. Not knowing that she even existed. The *janeu*, which I consciously hid at my own university, was on defiant display at JNU.

My wrestler-brethren engulfed me, protecting me from being recognized. They knew they were a dying breed, the desi *pehelwaan*. Most belonged to impoverished upper-caste families. They could wrestle in the mud and die in it. Or they could be of use to the world. That way, they got to eat meat twice a day, have milk straight from the cow's udder, and an infinite supply of desi *ghee* to ingest or slather on themselves.

It was the simplest of choices to make. For it wasn't much of a choice at all.

It gave them purpose, what they did. They were making a difference, ridding the nation of anti-nationals, saving its culture, saving the Gods. It was a noble line of work.

The ten seconds were a refuge. Draining, exhilarating. It quietened them for a few hours. Nobody discussed it after. They just needed the ten seconds when things got bad. And things were always bad.

I did not get the appeal then. The need. The addiction. I would, later, when things *really* got bad. I would see past the optical illusion. And once I did, I wouldn't be able to unsee it.

It would clean with fire what I did to Paro. How I lost her. And the Fight Club, with its ten seconds of peace, would be the nothingness I would long for. My addiction. My personal heaven.

The pain would become a welcome change from the guilt. The rush of endorphins would replace anything I ever felt. The lack of fear would be the lack of all feeling.

Until the day I would descend the steps of the *akhada*. Bloodied. Disoriented. Suicidal. Into the embrace of the only girl that ever truly loved me.

11

SWADESHI

Paro

I had grown used to those chairs. You know, the ones at the railway station, made of metal and deliberate neglect? Designed to be slanted, slippery, *uncomfortable*. So that no one could sit for too long, or God forbid, attempt to sleep on them. Well, I had been fidgeting on them for a decade, ever since the Mukherjees took me in. While *they* sat on wooden benches that were inviting, designed to keep you from falling. Those benches had pedigree. They had been donated by Shri Someone Important. It said so in white paint.

The absence of money wasn't something I was new to, yet it hadn't quite hit me the way it did in Jamia. Without

Dev *da* paying for both of us, the world felt a little smaller. Sanctioned, so to speak. I was expected to socialize, to hold a conversation over a plate of momos I couldn't afford. How does one do that, discuss something with someone like an equal, when one so clearly isn't?

I could have declined going out altogether, refused to meet my batchmates, saved myself from being recognized as unequal. But that was a luxury I couldn't afford. Moreover, I had grown up watching the Professor.

He was a spider, spinning thin, barely existent threads that led to other insects. He didn't mean to eat them, no. It was just so that he knew where they were, what they were capable of. So that when needed, he could use the silky threads to reach out, take whatever he could extract from them, and live to see another day. That's how he survived the scandal. That was his privilege.

And so I met insects and socialized in perpetual discomfort. One day, maybe, I too would have the license to fuck a minor and simply crawl to a different thread on my web. If it meant I'd have to endure endless debates on matters I had no stake in, I'd endure that. The insects worried about things other than themselves. That was another luxury I could not afford.

I sat with them as they worked themselves up into a frenzy, diagnosing the problems of the world over *chai*, *sutta* and beer. From Palestine to Kashmir, from the GDP to potholes, there was not a problem they didn't know the cause of. Solving it was altogether a different matter, though. They'd need something a little stronger than beer for that.

Sometimes, it felt like I was surrounded by ten Angry Little Devs.

In the weeks after the JNU incident, there was no discussion that didn't come back to it. If you had told me one of those discussions was going to change my life, I would've said there was some bad juju in your *ganja.*

'The VC has just asked the government to install a battle tank on the JNU campus.' Half of us scowled, while the other half laughed. I didn't know what was better, so I hid my face behind the menu. We were in Hauz Khas Village, in a brand-new rooftop café which was trying to disguise itself as old and vintage.

'*There's too much western influence*, that's what the government-spokesperson-fucktard said on the news last night!' Most of them were scowling this time, so I lowered the menu and joined in.

'Did you hear?' an Angry Little Dev chimed in. 'The *chaddis* have begun a Swadeshi movement. Buying only Indian products. To protect our *culture.*'

'And guess who that's going to benefit?' asked an Angry Little Dev. He didn't let anyone guess. 'The Bushy Businessman Baba, who else?'

There was a general hmmm-ing around the table. We all knew who he was talking about. The poster-boy of *desi* entrepreneurship. The monk who sold everything and became a billionaire.

'Mark my words: this misplaced nationalism is going to lead to protectionism and a closed economy. And the worst sufferers will be the ones already battling the disadvantages of intersectionality.'

There were too many 'isms' and 'ities' to disagree with the statement. We hmmm-ed some more.

'I heard the Left has called for a boycott of Swadeshi.'

'Sounds like a plan.' The Angry Little Devs were happy. There was silence. I flipped through the menu, scanned the sophisticated surroundings, and shuffled my feet.

Try as I might, I never felt like I belonged in these places. With these people. Food I couldn't pronounce, drinks I couldn't keep down, prices I couldn't afford, music I couldn't repeat the words to, with people I couldn't talk to.

Everything designed to exclude people like me. Slipping from the chair that didn't want me, fidgeting, trying to regain balance. I could have tolerated that, maybe, but that wasn't the extent of it. Everything was designed to *point me out*. A Spotlight, right on my ugliest body part. Misshapen, freaky, pitiful.

When I spoke, it was to distract them from noticing it.

'The Left supported Swadeshi, you know,' I remarked, 'under the British rule. Student leaders in Kolkata boycotted British goods.'

They stared at me, scandalized. Well distracted from the Spotlight.

'The British were the establishment, then, it's the conservatives now. And if they are intent on using Swadeshi as a means to curb the freedom of expression and get rich doing it, I say we oppose it.' Angry Little Dev was angry.

'The Right believes in free market, right? Isn't a closed economy against their ideology?' I remembered something from the Professor's ramblings.

'That's the economic Right, we're talking about the cultural Right!'

I shut up. There was no point arguing further. The Spotlight was gone; eyebrows would be raised over my politically incorrect notions, not because I couldn't order from the menu. *That* I was okay with.

The conversation left me wondering, though. I had never known that revolutions could be profitable. I had had the wrong teacher in the Professor. The Bushy Businessman Baba was a much better example. If there was indeed a Swadeshi movement brewing, there was opportunity brewing with it.

If the monk was selling the idea of nationalist pride, he would need somewhere to buy it from. And I knew just the place. Home Sweet Home. Haryana, *muddhas*, nylon wires and old tyres. Culturally appropriate furniture appropriated for the greater good. Made in India to boot.

I thought of the poor little artisans, toiling all day, with little to show for it, while the Western goliaths gobbled up the market. I couldn't let that happen anymore. They needed to have their piece of the pie. So did I. God willed it.

There was one problem, though. I was an Outsider. I couldn't convince my own kin, let alone the entire community. So I did the next best thing.

I went out and convinced someone who *wanted* to be convinced by me. Apparently, Bhuvan Chaudhary wasn't only skilled in covering up murders of caste-traitors. He knew how to exploit Men to make money. In the second-most populous country in the world, that's an incredibly valuable skill to possess.

He trusted me, for some reason. Maybe it was my fancy education. Maybe it was the fact that I had lived in two more metropolitans than he had. Maybe he just *wanted* to trust me. Whatever the reason, he was willing to bet the future of his people on my plan.

We collected some of the best handcrafted pieces of furniture from the village, loaded it on to a truck, and brought it to an ashram belonging to the billionaire monk. We left without the valuable inventory, but with an invitation to the first National Swadeshi Exhibition the coming month.

If I could pull it off, the Mukherjees would own me no longer. I wouldn't be real estate, invested in and landscaped to the owner's liking. I would be a person.

Free to want.

'You've done a good job here, Paro.'

I raised my head from the logbook to see Bhuvan smiling down at me. Behind him, the Ramlila Maidan was choked with legions of Bushy Baba's followers.

I smiled back. I couldn't remember the last time I'd been praised for something.

'It seems the stock is nearly sold out.' He remarked, looking at my rather empty stall.

'Oh, no. There wasn't enough space to display larger pieces, and that's where the real margins are. So, I made a catalogue—and took orders.'

I showed him more than three dozen customers I had accrued since the morning. Swadeshi was turning out to be a real money-spinner for us.

Bhuvan nodded. '*Babaji* is a crowd-puller, that's for sure.'

I saw the man himself, the Bushy Baba, up on the stage, jovially, teasingly encouraging people to help the nation by buying his products. I could've kissed his hairy, manic face in that moment.

Something distracted me, though. There were people standing behind him. His disciples, bodyguards, or just real avid shoppers, I didn't know. Amongst them was Devdas. He looked like he was bored, until he caught my gaze, startled, and rushed down the stage towards me.

'Can you look after the stall for a bit?' I asked Bhuvan. 'I'll be right back.'

The saffron clothes on Devdas's back were bright, bordering on fluorescent. Any other day he would have been a traffic cone on a dark road, but right now, he was indistinguishable from the crowd.

I squinted, trying to locate him again, when he tapped me on the shoulder. I jumped with glee and trapped him in an embrace.

'Where the hell have you been, idiot?' I screamed at him. 'I haven't seen you for months! You forgot I existed or what?' I had missed him terribly, now that I allowed myself to think about it.

'You mind explaining yourself?' he demanded, ignoring my outburst. 'What do you think you're doing here? The fuckers up there are taking the fanatics down there for a ride. Don't tell me you intend to spend your money here?'

What money? He sometimes forgot I had none.

'I am here selling, not buying.' I gestured towards my stall.

His eyes widened, scandalized, glaring in the direction I was pointing.

'You're *part* of this charade?' he whispered.

'Aren't you?' I stared at his clothes. 'If I didn't know any better, I would have thought you were rebelling against the Professor. What exactly are you doing on the stage?'

'This?' he was nonchalant. 'It's just an act. A means to an end. But you? This is no place for a rational, thinking human being. These fuckers are intent on forcing the same patriarchal, *savarna* structures on us that they have for hundreds of years—'

'On *us*?' I raised an eyebrow. 'Neither of us are Dalits, if I remember correctly.'

'That's not the point!' he exclaimed, holding my shoulders with an iron grip. I forget the number of times I had deliberately pissed him off just for a morsel of a physical touch, even if it was painful at times.

'So, what is the point?' I challenged him. 'I am just making some money. For me, too, it's a means to an end.' *You.*

His grip loosened in shock. 'You're doing this for a bit of cash?' he gasped. 'I never thought—a capitalist in my own house—why would you—why?'

I don't know what came over me; probably the fact that I had *earned* something today, something that was not *given* to me. It was strange and liberating and euphoric. Like a fool, I believed the day had come when I could *want*.

'So that you don't feel responsible for me. So that I don't feel indebted to you.'

He was flummoxed, not quite understanding what I meant. 'Come again?'

I had left it unsaid for so long, I didn't know if I could, finally. I knew I had to, though. I had been homesick since we came to Delhi. I had hoped Haryana would cure it, but it had not. The homesickness didn't go away—not until Devdas came and tapped me on the shoulder.

'I am in love with you.' The words left my lips, trembling in fear and uncertainty. The words, not my lips. 'I have been for years.'

He chuckled, slightly disarmed. 'I love you, too, kiddo,' he ruffled my hair. I hated it when he acted like he was older than me. I hated that he wasn't taking it seriously.

'You're my home, Devdas.' It took every ounce of courage and foolishness within me, but I did say it.

He cleared his throat, taking a step back. 'Come on, Paro,' he muttered, 'you're joking, right?'

I smouldered, hurt. 'What makes you think I am joking right now?'

'I can't be with you!' he seemed horrified at the thought. 'We're—we're—' he was grasping for a reason as a rational, thinking human being, 'we're both Brahmins, for God's sake!'

I gulped down my pride, put it in the pit of my stomach, and asked the question that didn't matter any more.

'What has that got to do with it?' I dared him to give me a reason to hate him, I *hoped* he'd give me a reason to hate him. That's the only way I could survive this.

'Look. You're not any other girl, all right? We can't just have a thing and move on. You would want more.' He was rambling, breathless. 'You would want a life together. You would want marriage, and that's something we *must not* do. We can't propagate the Brahmanical superiority myth. Upper-castes have a duty towards subversion. We must marry into other, unprivileged—'

I walked away. Slowly at first, then with a firmness and ease that surprised me. I couldn't let Devdas complete his train of thought and insult my love for him. It would remain untarnished, unlike my pride.

I took my position at the stall, ignoring Bhuvan's inquisitive stare. I knew my eyes were wet. And Devdas was the teardrop hanging on my eyelash. The weight of him was unbearable. I blinked, and he fell down. The weight was still unbearable because of what I carried within me—an infinite supply of tears.

I wiped it away for now, reminding myself that I was free to want. I just needed to want something other than him.

A customer stopped by. I smiled my widest smile.

'What are you looking for, sir?'

12

AZAADI

Chandramukhi

What's your name? is the most hostile question a common man can ask a government employee. Sounds like you're seeking vital information before lodging a complaint against them. A declaration of war. Doubly tricky if you actually come in peace.

The common man is resourceful, though, and almost as cunning as the government employee. He's got a workaround. I had learnt it while standing in cashier queues and admission windows. Just one additional word, and it makes it all okay.

'What is your good name?' I inquired, politely.

The jailer answered me, and armed with the information, I familiarized myself with him. Enough for him to open up and provide me other vital information about the prisoner I was visiting. My father.

As it turned out, the Dal boatman had become the number one masseuse in Tihar. In the last two decades, every VIP inmate who had passed through could attest to his skills. In here, he enjoyed an amount of protection and leniency reserved for good servants.

It didn't prepare me in any way. He was a stranger now. I stood in the long, narrow corridor, the long omnipresent metal mesh on either side, and leaned in like so many others.

'Chandramukhi?' a bearded old man inquired, his eyes frisking me, suspicious. He smelled like coconut oil.

I nodded, uncertain. I couldn't recognize him, even when I pressed my cheeks into the mesh, and my left eye got an unfiltered vision of him. I could almost forget that he was behind bars, but I couldn't remember him at all.

'How—how have you been?'

He blinked. 'No one's asked me that in years.'

I didn't doubt that. And suddenly it struck me. He might've been responsible for the death of half-a-dozen people; he might've been a terrorist. In here, he was just a lonely old man. There seemed to be an epidemic of them.

'I was innocent, you know. They framed me.' His voice turned acidic in a way that I could almost taste. I couldn't quite place it. Was the taste sour or bitter? And what was the difference between the two?

'Sure,' I said convincingly. He chuckled sharply.

'Your mother never believed me either.'

I wanted to believe him. 'So, you didn't place the bomb, then?'

'What do I know about bombs?' he raised his hands upwards. 'I knew the people that did it. I rowed them across the Dal. That's it.'

'Did you know who they were when you helped them?'

His gaunt face was like a barren mountain of stone, with valleys and peaks on his cheeks. His eyes were earnest as he leaned in.

'Living as we did … under the rule that we did … our people helped each other. Isn't that how you found me? One of us brought you to your father.'

'Where were you when mother and I needed help? Where were the rest of *us*?'

'It was necessary to raise our voices, Chandramukhi. Bit by bit, we have made the world care—'

'Do you think people who *aren't us* care about us? Do you think anybody cares about anybody else? Do *you* care about anybody else?'

He stared at me, unable to find his tongue, disappointment in his eyes. That's when I knew … I was a stranger to him as well.

'Are you saying you have no interest in correcting the wrongs done to our people?' It was an accusation.

'I don't.' I pitied his naivety and forgave his faith. I supposed he had to cling on to something all this while. He needed to believe the cause was worth it, worth losing his family over.

'Then why did you join the Comrades and pretend you wanted to fight? Why are you here, after all this while?'

'I am searching for *ammi*.'

'What—wait—is she not with you?' he seemed clouded. 'Your mother stopped writing or visiting years ago. I thought she had stopped seeing the point of it.'

'She just disappeared one night. No one knows what happened to her. If she's alive or …' I let it hang in the air longer than I should have. My father looked panicked, and half-clasped the metal mesh with his fingers, mistaking it for a doorknob that'd turn and let him look for his wife. He must've remembered where he was, for he let his grip loosen.

'This is not Kashmir. How can someone just disappear—'

'You know what line of work she was in, don't you?' I was horrified I'd have to break it to him. He waited, expectant. I gulped. 'She was a … a … in G.B. Road.'

Tears flowed through the peaks and valleys on my father's face. He turned the topography away from me, hiding it in shadows.

'The Uniforms said she must've gone with the wrong customer one night. Lost to the vagaries of her profession. They never found her body, though. I thought maybe she just got fed up, and managed to get out … contacted you …'

He turned back to me, hunched in fear and anticipation like an animal hunted in the wild. 'What happened to you after she went missing, Chandramukhi?' There was anguish in his voice. Pleading, praying for no more truth. 'Please. Tell me the truth, daughter.'

I could either tell him about my suffering or spare him his. The choice was an easy one. I brushed his hand on the partition between us. 'I was lucky. The policemen got me out, put me in an orphanage. I found a—a mentor of sorts. I go to college, and stay on campus.'

He exhaled out the tension within him, able to face me again. 'I am thankful for that. I always worried if I'd be able to give you an education. Now you have one. The Indians cannot fool you like they fooled us. Treat you like cattle as they treated us.'

We were back to that.

'I told you, Father. I am not interested in any of that. I've seen too much of right and wrong, black and white, Right and Left; people refusing to walk the tightrope in the middle, afraid that they'll fall on the wrong side. Yet, I have also seen a Nepali, a Bangladeshi, a Kashmiri, a Sikh and a Hindu live in the same house, work for the same pimp—united by the fact that each of them needed to eat, and by their willingness to get screwed every day to be able to. Because of your *cause*, I was destined to join them. By some miracle and the kindness of strangers, I have a life. I intend to live it.'

'Live it for what?'

'For whom,' I corrected him. 'Myself.'

He gnashed his teeth, trying to make me understand. 'You must have a cause, my love. You must have purpose. And those that do are the ones who make a difference. The ones who stop and point the bastards out.' A thought occurred to him that made him smile and mutter, 'We must stop the train.'

'The train?'

He took his time to answer. Unhurried, unmoved, thinking idly, as only a man who's stared at walls for years can. 'The train passenger is the ultimate neutral observer. He watches everything out of the window, insulated, silent. Watching the wrongs. Not saying anything. *We* are not like that. We pull the chain. We stop the train. We point them out. We shame them.'

He laughed and for a moment, I had my father back. Not a stranger, for I remembered the laugh as clear as the Valley's autumn. Then his eyes were blank again, mirthless, as he made his final, naïve joke.

'And one day, hopefully, they'll stop shitting on the tracks.'

13

SLAM

Devdas

You say she was chasing love,
Migration is trait of a turtledove.
I'll laugh. I'll shrug. I'll laugh some more.
Tell me another joke, just one more.
You say shit happened to her,
And I'll say she did shit, as it were.
Wherever she is, and whoever she is fucking,
I blame my mother squarely for this aching.
She left and it was just me and my dad,
Can't say how much, but I was hell'a mad.
To have and to lose, the love of your life,
I was too young to understand an after-life.

The Professor bore it well as he could,
Bore it a little better than he should.
For reasons known best to him,
He bought me a toy, *maybe* on a whim.
That's how I met my new sister,
We played, we fought. Oh, nothing sinister.
We were kids and we found together,
What the genders looked like down there.
I was irritable, she was double-jointed,
To help, to blame, at me she pointed.
A sun rose in the base of my thumbnail,
To me, her lips were astonishingly pale.
I really, really sucked at sports,
She just hated wearing shorts.
We discovered what together, and how!
I don't think I have the time to tell all, now.
Suffice to say I wound up my toy,
A good purchase, it brought me joy.
I learnt it was mine, and mine alone,
Unlike my mother, she'd mind her tone.
And when she didn't,
I could smack her around.
It reminded us both that she was mine alone,
And unlike my mother, she'd mind her tone.
I'd desired it since I was a boy,
The love of everyone, to enjoy,
My newly minted sister gave me that,
Which my father in time did retract.

With unconditional love I was complacent,
It stopped finally, the uneasy torment.
Older, love didn't cut it, I craved adoration,
I found it, I found it, but never to satiation.
Then came the day I feared would come,
I lost the second woman since my mum.
My toy had grown weary and broken apart,
And now I cling to my sorrow and my art.
I have three minutes of verse to share,
Before and after, a sea of despair.
She went ahead and was free of me,
I thought it was for a while, not eternity.
I was wrong as I was wrong throughout,
She had moved on; I had moved out.
I cursed my decision to be a fool,
Did that give her the right to be so cruel?
I am a shadow of my father's beliefs,
Shadows don't cry, need no kerchiefs.
In an attempt to win her back,
I ended up displaying all I lack.
I lack a spine and a soul,
All I could be was an ugly troll.
Strangely, it is pain that is my friend,
It is self-pity that gives a helping hand.
I am afraid I'll be addicted to sorrow,
For memories of my toy, it does borrow.
The times I hit her come to mind,
Why couldn't I have been more kind?

And now she's left me like my mother,
I'll piss at you if you talk of either.
I can't tell her who to and who not to fuck,
My father might be, but I'm not a cuck.
There's a decision to be made yet,
Since my toy and a new boy have met.
She makes money, he makes her laugh,
That son of a bitch took my best half.
She is perfect, I now see, in every way,
If she wasn't, she'd still have sway.
I'll find out for myself, one of these days,
If she'll burn alongside me in this blaze.
The temptation was strong,
The temptation was wrong.
To be, and to conquer,
To lose, and to shudder,
You need a brave heart inside you,
She has mine, with it she flew.
So, I'll cut her down from the sky today!
And unlike my whore mother, she *won't* fly away …

14

THE MARK

Paro

The thing with being hurt by someone you love is you force yourself to believe that this time is going to be the last. No, this time. Okay, okay, this time …

Every time.

Something had happened when I was little. Something I am forgetting. It was the day I had lost ownership of my body. Devdas had taken something from me. He had got punished, of course, but the deed was done.

What had he taken? Maybe the answer would come to me some day in a half-dream, half-memory …

It was a little hard to discern where I ended, and Devdas began. We had been inseparable for so long. Fused, somehow. And I couldn't pry myself away.

It was as if I'd put my hand on something sticky, and I didn't want to remove it. As long as my hand was on that tenacious substance, I could ignore the stickiness. But the moment I withdrew from it, I would *need* to wash it off. So that's how I stayed for years—in a stalemate. And when I finally had the courage to pull away, Devdas clung to me like the icky-sticky thing he was. Our atoms had fused; some weird osmosis. It had been too long to simply wash him off.

Not that I didn't try.

As soon as I was done counting the cash I'd made at the nationalist fair, I made the only logical decision I had made regarding my love-life. Not that it had anything to do with love. I got engaged to Bhuvan the Bulky Brahmin. It'd help me consolidate my newfound enterprise. That it might also piss Devdas off was just a lucky coincidence.

Bhuvan found my education and ambition fascinating, otherworldly. Like a unicorn. He encouraged it, preserved it. That he helped cover up murders of the Dishonourable was just an unlucky titbit.

He didn't know anything about dating. He didn't know how to court someone. So he just stated his intention matter-of-factly. Would I, if I wasn't already betrothed, consider marrying him? He would get my parents' permission. He would need no dowry. His family would be happy and intimidated enough with a nice, educated girl. As long as she was a Brahmin.

I searched for a reason to say no. I couldn't find it, so I said yes. The Professor disapproved of such a step at an age so young, but he didn't assume the authority to tell me how to live my life. I wish he had. I might have acquiesced to his wishes in order to repay him a little bit.

Devdas was another matter, though. He wouldn't take it lying down. I knew exactly how he would react. And sure enough, I found him waiting outside my class at Jamia one day, bursting at the seams from righteous anger.

No, I won't go into it. I won't say what he said. I'll just say that he didn't find the prospect of me marrying a Brahmin particularly appealing. I'll just say that he didn't think I was much of a feminist. I'll just say that he had reconsidered and was generously willing to take me back with open arms. He said he loved me, too …

The icky-sticky thing clung to me, and even though I knew I couldn't, I did try to wash it off.

I did what I do best. I made fake tears erupt and pointed the finger at him. I tore through his façade. I humiliated him—with an audience. The Jamia fellows knew of him. They saw the rising poet go down with his reputation. Trying to intimidate a lonely little girl? I'll say they didn't think *he* was much of a feminist, either.

Someone recorded my tirade, unfortunately. *Pinjra Tod*'s martyr had been caught slut-shaming his sister. The slam poet was a traitor. The little birdies went after him with a vengeance, trending *#SlamSexists* for a day on Twitter.

Poor old Devdas was too woke to be able to have a good night's sleep after that. I had even called him a possessive communist. Now, there's an oxymoron.

I had believed—rather naïvely, now that I look back on it—that that laid the matter to rest.

I was half-asleep. I was only half-dreaming.

I am nine. I love my hair. I know hair is the only difference between girls and boys. These are the most important facts of life. Irrefutable.

I was seventeen. I was an entrepreneur. Devdas didn't love me. I was engaged to be married. These were the most important facts of life. My hair didn't matter much, for some strange reason.

I am lying on the cot in my little room. My little room is inside the Professor's home. Afternoon has paralyzed the city into laziness. I'm in Kolkata.

I was lying on my bed in my room. My room was in the Professor's home. Not for long, though. I was an entrepreneur. I was in Delhi.

Dev bhaiya is angry with me. He showed me his, but I didn't show him mine. Now I know hair isn't the only difference between boys and girls.

Am I sleeping? Or just pretending to? My eyes are closed.

I haven't heard from Devdas for quite a while. Not since the fiasco. Not since I rejected him. It was a blissful feeling that turned bitter in my mouth.

Was I asleep? Or only half-asleep? My eyes were closed. I was having a dream, or a memory.

I hear light footsteps on the ground. Approaching me. He whispers my name. 'Paro.' I pretend not to hear.

I heard a slight rustling as someone entered the room. I knew who it was. I recognized the footsteps. I smiled. It was him again, coming to say sorry. To tell me we were meant to be together.

Wasn't that how the memory ended?

SNIP. My eyes open in horror. He's grinning crookedly. He's holding scissors in one hand, and my beautiful braid of hair in the other. I reach around, and my palm finds my naked neck.

I remembered it all, now. The footsteps grew nearer still. I didn't open my eyes. I knew he was coming to say sorry. I knew the memory was just a memory. He had changed. When he said he didn't love me, he had hurt me for the last time. He would never hurt me again. I just knew it.

A gentle splash. A warm fluid flooded my face and neck. My eyes opened in confusion. Devdas was already scurrying out of the window, the little glass vial still in his hand. It was empty. Its erstwhile contents were corroding my very being right now.

I had been naïve. I had been hopeful. The acid would wash that out forever.

My skin screamed first. Then I did.

15

THE MARK

Chandramukhi

At first, I thought the scream was Happy, and mine. I was in the Professor's room, under his thrusting, flailing, selfish body. He stopped. The screaming did not.

By the time we reached Paro's room upstairs, she was on the floor, writhing. The Professor called out to her, but I knew that in this moment, she couldn't see or hear us. She'd have no sense of memory, or smell. All she had right now, was the misfortune to *feel*.

Her hands scrambled for the jug of water as she poured its contents—which were exhausted in a cruelly infinitesimal second—over her face. The Professor was rooted to the spot. All his knowledge, all his wisdom crept down him, slithering away on the floor. I pushed him aside and guided-dragged Paro to the bathroom, placing her under running tap water.

I knew what had happened. I had seen the aftermath once or twice back in Paharganj. Faces melted off, hanging off their former selves as an angry rub of birthday cake. I had heard their stories. Strangely, though, none of them wanted to talk about how it *felt*. I now knew why. Living through it once had been enough.

Paro kept screaming through the curtain of water, struggling against my grip. But I kept her there against her will, long enough for her to stop struggling, long enough for the Professor to find his feet and his car keys. By the time we were on our way to the hospital, Paro's screams had subsided to guttural sounds of pain and fear.

'We're almost there, Paro,' I whispered, 'it'll be all right.'

It would not be all right. It would never be all right again.

At the hospital, the doctors didn't need explanations, the nurses didn't need instructions. They just wordlessly got to work, a cruel efficiency that comes with practice. None of them were horrified, none of them were surprised. This was routine. Paro was just another face. Or what was left of it.

'This was in your house?' the Uniform was drawling.

The Professor nodded.

'She was upstairs?'

The Professor nodded.

'You were downstairs?'

We nodded. The Uniform pointed at me.

'Who's she?'

'A student.'

A considered pause. Then a shrug.

'Who did it?'

The Professor exhaled. Then mirrored the shrug.

'The window was open,' I contributed.

'Any threats? Any jilted lovers?'

Both of us shook our heads. Both of us, I suppose, were being honest.

The Uniform left us to go and talk to the doctor. Paro, luckily, was under sedation right now. Her mind needed time. To register the trauma. To catch up with her body. And in time, both would be equally scarred.

The eloquent Professor hadn't spoken a word since we'd found his ward. He had made calls to his son, who did not pick up. The silence, thus, remained unbroken.

My body couldn't bear the stillness. It needed to catch up with my mind, it needed unrest. I got up and started pacing. There was something comforting about a hospital; it reminded me that the unfairness stopped at some point. By the time it ended, everyone's life was a tragedy.

I stopped. I had seen something, something familiar.

An owl.

Embossed on the back of a man's shirt, the owl leaned towards me, its eyes wide, unflinching, following me. A group of owls was called a parliament. I don't know why I remembered that.

I moved closer. The man was talking to a woman who was dinged up pretty good, bandages covering most of her bare skin. I imagined this is what Paro would soon look like.

I tapped the man on the shoulder, who spun around, making the owl turn its back on me.

'Excuse me. Can you tell me who you work for? The logo … on the back of your shirt.'

He immediately took out a card and handed it to me. 'It's an NGO, madam. We work in areas of human trafficking and sexual exploitation. We're always watching,' he pointed at the owl.

I thanked him and walked away. I remembered, now, where I had seen it before.

The owl had come to free me and my mother, all those years ago. It had failed, of course. I doubt a bird has ever freed someone from the jaws of the saltwater crocodile. Not unless it was prepared to pierce its eyes with its beak. This miracle required doing, not just watching.

We're always watching. I had heard that before, too. Somebody really ought to tell them that owls slept.

Despite experience, despite myself, and despite what I had witnessed today, I felt the uncomfortable nudge of hope in my impatient breath. I had found another link to my mother. I'd get to know what became of her.

And if the answer wasn't too horrible, maybe, just maybe, I would stop hearing her screams.

16

THUD. THUD. THUD

Devdas

Well, fuck.

Don't you judge me. Don't say it. Is my cock out and in front of your face? No, right? Then shut your mouth.

I did it. I marked her mine, forever. I knew she deserved it; I knew she could take it. Women handle pain better than us. Any real feminist knows that.

Then why was I feeling what I was feeling? I ran through the crowded streets of Old Delhi, my feet operating from muscle memory, leading me to my place of refuge. I wasn't mad at what I did, I suppose. I was mad at having run away.

I did the right thing, right? Then why did I run? I was on the moral high ground—by the way, why do they call it moral *science*? Is it so methodical, that cut and dry?

I didn't think Paro would mind, honestly. That was the sort of relationship we had. She had let me do it so many times before. I had her consent. At least I think I did.

Some say consent must be taken over and over again, others say once it's given, it's given until you withdraw it. Right now, I was leaning towards the latter. Paro never withdrew hers, right? The last time I hurt her, she didn't say I no longer could.

Aah! Murky waters, surely. There's no correct answer. Like the metaphysician's dilemma of why there is something rather than nothing. Like the husband's confusion about leaving the toilet seat up or down.

The thing is, it never seems like I am done pissing. So, the seat stays perennially up.

My feet stopped. I saw it. The door to my salvation. The door to the *akhada*.

I removed my shirt and bared my *janeu*. No one stopped me. I motioned the nearest meathead to the centre of the sandpit. Chunni would be happy, I was playing the part he wanted me to play. The reformed Brahmin.

THUD. A closed fist rankled against my skull. On the ground, spitting out sand, I smiled. Finally, I felt something else than what I had been feeling.

I got back up and ran into the meathead head-on. He put me in a chokehold and rammed his elbow against my spine. WHAM.

I screamed in agony. It only made it worse. Not only was I reminded of Paro's wailing, but the meathead grew a conscience and stopped beating on me.

I snarled and went at him again. We scuffled. CRACK. Something broke in my jeans pocket. I knew what it was. The broken glass clawed against my thigh, scraping the skin, and the remaining drops of acid corroded their way into the tissue. I screamed in euphoria, purified. I was feeling a bit of what Paro must be feeling.

I hadn't stayed, that was my shame, but now … I was with her.

I was still with *her* when I realized that I was with Chandramukhi. I had been sewn up and put back together. The searing pain was gone, and the shame was back. I opened my eyes and looked at her sleeping next to me. Not *her*, her.

Chandramukhi's face was inches from mine, eyes shut, lost in another world. I don't know if it was sheer exhaustion from dragging me across Paharganj to her loft, but I envied her carefree slumber.

I don't know how, but she sensed me thinking about her, for her eyes opened the next moment.

'How're you feeling now?' she muttered with intimacy that we didn't have. Probably a part of her job, making men feel loved.

'You've wasted your time on me,' I mumbled. 'I don't pay for sex.'

'Oh, I think you've paid enough,' she smirked, unhurt, unfrazzled.

I sat up straight, sore.

'How're you feeling?' she asked again.

'Good,' I said. *Too good.* Better than *her.* And that seemed wrong.

I tried to get up, and collapsed back on to the cot, head spinning.

'You can stay here until you feel better,' she offered.

I thought about it. Where would I go? Not back to that house again. I imagined smelling her burnt flesh.

'What about your customers?'

She chuckled. 'Let me worry about my customers. You better lie down now …'

She moved to gently push me to lie back down. I jumped as if scalded by her touch.

'I won't touch you if that's what you want,' she said simply, unperturbed, unoffended.

She didn't understand. I couldn't take her touch, not because she was a prostitute, not because I was disgusted by her. I was disgusted *for* her, by myself. How could I let her touch something so slimy, so yuck?

'What's your name?'

She smiled and didn't say, 'Chandramukhi.'

I nodded and didn't say, 'Devdas.'

She didn't stop me from going to the *akhada* when I got better. Neither did she stop me from coming back to collapse in her bed afterwards. I never asked the reason for her kindness, and she never offered any. She disappeared for hours while I slept, and I never asked her how much she made a night.

We were strangers and knew nothing about each other. We were whatever the other thought we were. I was the wounded bird, and she was the hooker with a heart of gold.

At times when neither of us was sleeping or being pounded by our chosen tormentors, we talked. Hours on end. Occasionally, she would read from her favourite book, a yellowing, stolen library copy of *Devdas.* I didn't pay much attention to her words, for it was her voice that was a balm. Calming, soothing, healing. Better than her First Aid skills. Calling me Devdas, christening me with a name that had a sad ending.

She would put me back together, and then my craving would return. I would have to go back to the sand pit and get my face bashed in again, to be with *her* again. And I would come back, limping, to her.

She never asked me why I did what I did, why I punished myself. It would have been a pointless thing to ask, anyway. As pointless as the housewife asking the plumber in porn,

'Oh my … what are you doing?' He was unzipping his pants, madam. He was doing what he was *supposed* to do. He was getting to the fucking.

There was one question she did ask me, though.

'You do know you're going to kill yourself like this?'

Of course, I knew. The how, the when, I was a bit murky on.

I hate an incomplete story. The ending is so important, the final act. Without it, all you have are possibilities. That's depressing. You have the right to know how your hero died.

Take the Bard of Avon, for instance. The greatest playwright in the history of civilization, and they don't know how he died. Something about a fever, something about an illness, and bam! The End.

It may have been sinister, like his tragedies. It may have been superfluous, like his comedies. No one stored the information for posterity, convinced in the fleeting nature of his existence. After all, what's in a name?

It's not like I am comparing myself to the Bard, but if I was comparing myself to the Bard, I'd say there was not much of a comparison. Dying in ignominy was not my fate. Which, I found out, was not necessarily a good thing.

I think you've earned the right to know the ending of my story. Once I tell you, I can finish the rest of it in relative peace. In fact, I already did tell you. Were you paying attention? Do you know how I died?

On the Inside, kicked by a Small One, wrinkling my nose at the prospect of being *Ban-gaal*. My last memory was a foot swinging in a perfect arc, an arc that had my face in its trajectory. The last word I heard, thankfully, didn't misidentify me. *Bhadralok*.

That was me, to the very end.

A distinguished gentleman.

17

QUID PRO QUO

Paro

I woke up, empty. The pain wasn't fully gone yet. The memory of it, I knew, would never be fully gone.

The Professor was by my side. His eyes were red, and his hands were shaking. He noticed me move a little in my hospital bed, and his eyes widened—in hope and in dread.

'Are you in pain, Paro?' he fidgeted around, looking for help. 'Should I call the nurse?'

I had never seen him so helpless. He was just a man, after all.

I shook my head lightly. 'Did they catch him?'

His eyes lost hope. There was only dread now.

'Him?' he asked, unconvincingly. 'Who?'

I would have smirked if my face wasn't hidden from him under the bandages.

'Dev.'

The Professor gulped. See, Dev always believed his father didn't give two hoots about him. I knew better.

'What are you saying?' the Professor said, very much aware of what I was saying. 'What's Dev got to do with this?'

'Everything.' I pushed a button on my left. A nurse came sauntering in. 'Can you call the police?' I asked politely. 'I'd like to give my statement.'

She left. The Professor stayed. The pretence was gone.

'I am sorry, I am sorry,' he whispered. 'I am sorry for bringing you to him.'

'Where is he hiding, Professor?'

He closed his eyes. 'Chandramukhi.'

'So, she was another one of your protégés? That time she dropped me at the house—'

'We had known each other for years.'

'How come Dev's with her?'

'She just … took him in.'

'Why?'

'I don't know, I didn't ask her to.' He paused for a moment, betraying a slight hint of wonder. 'Maybe … she took in *Devdas*.'

'*Devdas*?'

'That's what she calls him.'

Weirder things had happened, so I let it go.

'And now he's staying with her,' I noted. The girl had spirit. First the heavenly father, then the holy son.

'He's … he's in really bad shape, Paro, he's in a lot of pain—'

At this, I had to laugh. It hurt, which made my point. The Professor broke off, hanging his head in shame.

'I am sorry,' he repeated, 'I am sorry for bringing you to him.'

'Why did you?' I said sharply. I could finally ask him the thing I'd wanted to know for years. 'What made you take a girl from her family, and use her to sustain yours?'

'No good deed …' He let his voice trail off, then collected his courage. 'I had driven his mother away, and it was just the two of us. I wanted—I *needed* to show my son that his father wasn't all bad. So, I took him on a journey. I was going to change the world, help people, make lives better, and my son was going to watch—and remember. I needed him to know his father was a good man.'

'And you failed.'

'Yes. Who knew the country wasn't ready to change? Anyone who wasn't an idealist, I guess, but that wasn't me. I accomplished nothing in the year we spent running from her memory.'

'And me?'

Professor Narayan Mukherjee half-smiled and looked at me with something akin to affection. 'You were my one good deed. Your family was in cyclical poverty. There was a good chance that you wouldn't survive adolescence. So,

I did what I had to. I chose to show my son my one good deed.'

I did not know whether to laugh or to cry. I leaned towards him and scraped a piece of the bandage off my face, to bare the skin. It was painful, but I could bear it. This was the just the tail of the pain; I had been through the entire monster.

'What does your good deed look like *now*, Professor?'

Devdas was a sinking ship, but even a sinking ship comes to rest at the bottom of the ocean. It is the people aboard who pay the real price: the passengers, the captain ... the stowaway.

I paid my price. I had got off too late, but I had got off at last.

In the days that followed, I had ample time to appreciate exactly what I had lost, other than my face. For most of my life, my love for Dev was the only real thing I felt, the only good thing. I loved him and that made me love myself. It is exhilarating to find oneself capable of such unadulterated emotion. And now, it was over.

I had lost the ability to love. Myself. Or anyone else. I had spent it all, on *him*. And there hadn't been enough to begin with. Just like singing happy birthday to someone with a monosyllabic name. It just doesn't feel right. It doesn't fit. Try it. Happy birthday to you, Happy birthday to you, Happy birthday to dear D–eee–eeee–ev! See? Not enough of it to last.

Not for that affection-starved, motherless street-dog. I had made the mistake of making tch-tch-tch noises to it. We both mistook each other's love to be unconditional, but only I paid the price. I had its dirty paws all over me. I needed to get clean. I needed to free myself.

So when Bhuvan came to me, I was prepared, fully expecting his bristling rage and righteous vendetta. He didn't ask how I was doing. He didn't ask if I was comfortable. All he wanted to know was the name of the person who did this to me.

He needed to get even, I suppose.

I had a feeling that he wouldn't have ended our engagement had I given him the name. I chose not to. He was smart enough to guess that I was protecting my assailant. He was foolish enough to believe that I was doing it out of love.

'I can live with the mark he left on your face. I can't live with the one he left on your heart.' At least, I guess that's what Bhuvan might have said—if only he had learnt to communicate with women as well as he had learnt to bury them. He did say that the wedding was off.

I didn't mind. I had nothing left to give him. Although there was plenty I still intended to take.

Once they found time to pay me a visit, the policemen asked me for the name as well. Having kept the Professor in suspense for all this time, I told them the same thing I had told my former fiancée. I didn't know.

The Professor was by my side, holding his breath. He didn't say it, but he willed me to know to keep his son out of it. When the policemen left without a name, Narayan Mukherjee looked at me with gratitude.

I didn't say it, but I *willed* him to know, like I did, that my debt was finally paid.

18

WHORES DON'T DIE

Chandramukhi

'... after that, after that she had no chance. She was ... disappeared.' The old lady tried to be comforting, without noticing the cruel irony of her words. Something my Kashmiri father hadn't missed. Mother had brought us to Delhi to avoid being *disappeared*.

We sat in her living room, which bore witness to a life that had more important things in it than fixing seepage and faded paint.

'Did they beat her?' I asked, my throat constricted.

She was hardened by a life witnessing pain, one without paint. She didn't hesitate.

'Yes. She came here, afterwards. Broken ribs, internal and external bleeding, delirious. Kept saying she needed to go get her kid. She was gone by the next morning … never saw or heard of her after that. I went to the *thana*, but you know what the law is like in these cases.'

Of course, I did. I came from a place where the law was designed to screw you. It had been a while before I understood that all places were like the place I came from.

'I remember you—I think,' I said softly, 'you brought me—books. With that logo on them. That's where I kept seeing the owl.'

'Education got me out,' she said. 'I just passed it on.'

'You were a prostitute?'

'A sex worker,' she corrected me.

I kept mum.

'She's not dead, you know,' the lady remarked. 'Not really.'

'I thought they killed her and dumped her somewhere. Can you be more dead?'

'Sure, you can. I have seen it. Women who once *were*, simply gone. After a while, not a trace of them having existed. No one missed them. Not their customers, not their pimps. No family to speak of. Just up in the ether.'

'You remember them, though, that ought to count for something.' Strangely, *I* was trying to console *her*.

'I am *haunted* by them,' she said with a grimace, 'there's a difference.'

'And my mother?'

'Has a daughter who searches for her, who is grateful for her sacrifice. Think. Think of the last thing your mother wanted to do—see her daughter. Think of the only thing *you've* wanted to do since she left—find your mother.' The lady smiled, an all-knowing, toothless smile. 'And then tell me if she's really dead ...'

The seedy, Old Delhi cinema hall was submerged in darkness, as were the two lovers on the silver-screen, doing things to each other that they couldn't actually show—at least, not without having Uniforms raid the place. Not that they needed to be explicit, to be honest. Growing up in the country I did, I was well-trained in the art of deciphering what was being done to the heroine off-screen by no visual aid other than her expressions on-screen.

My powers of deduction were compromised right now, for I couldn't see, for I was crying, for I had learnt how my mother's story ended. The darkness afforded me some privacy, but not for long. I had a date with Devdas.

Between my sobs, I heard the buxom siren reaching orgasm in chaste Bhojpuri, and I imagined her expression. Devdas, late as usual, plopped down on the seat next to me. There were fresh bruises on his face; he was coming straight from the *akhada*. I smelt the blood. He heard the tears.

I hadn't told him about my mother. I hadn't told him so many things.

We stared at each other, and then I was on top of him. A messy mishmash of blood, sweat, tears, and other stuff. We were a heap of moans and groans. Some painful, some painfully pleasing. I leave the rest to the imagination. Crying at the movies is great, almost better than sex, but crying sex at the movies? Nothing tops that.

As I succumbed to Devdas's warmth, I promised myself something: I wouldn't die like my mother. I'd leave a family to mourn me. A husband, kids, people I worked with, people who admired me, people who pitied me. I'd leave a dead body, at least.

I wouldn't close myself up any more. I refused to live my life afraid of bad things *and* good things. I couldn't rely on the loneliness of Narayan Mukherjee to lessen mine. I'd rather rely on the love of his son.

Once the show was over, that's what I did. I went to the patron of my art and told him what's what. The Professor took it with the graciousness he had learnt from the failure of his marriage and wished me well. We grew nostalgic and laughed. We grew optimistic and sobered up. At the end, he asked me to take care of his son. I promised I would. He hesitated, and asked me to take care of myself. I didn't really get it, but I promised I would.

I was floating in the air on my way back home. My body was still in Devdas's arms, back in the cheap seats of the cinema hall. The electric motor of my scooter purred beneath my feet, echoing my silent excitement. There was an involuntary smile on my face.

I would be unable to bear the wait any longer, so I didn't. There were things that needed to be said to my lover, and I'd rather not say them to his face. I parked on the side of the road, and jumped up on the footpath, dialling his number. My heart skipped a beat as he picked up.

'What?'

My heart skipped a beat again. His tone was a blunt knife, prepared for repeated thrusts to get to the bone.

'I—I wanted to tell you—'

'That you're a whore?' His revulsion pushed my voice down my throat. 'I always knew that. What you hid, you two-faced, manipulative bitch—is that my father was a customer. I saw you together!'

I still couldn't speak. I couldn't believe we had been in each other's arms mere hours ago.

'I ended it,' I whispered. 'I went there to end it ... It's you, just you.'

'You're all the same.' He barked a laugh. 'I was a fool to expect anything different. A fucking whore. You deserve to live and die like one.'

CLICK.

That was the last thing I heard from him. I don't know when I stopped shaking, or got on my scooter, or managed to swerve through the by-lanes of Paharganj. Adding to its pungent smell.

The smell of Kashmiri willow is around me. I am under the tarpaulin of the goods truck. My head resting on my mother's lap, as we fled from our home. It would be dawn by the time we reached the station in Jammu. For now, it felt like being dunked in the Dal at night. Afraid to take a full breath or see through the darkness.

I entered the *haveli* and started walking up, dodging the Workers, hiding my face from them. One of them wanted to say something, maybe she did say it, but I was too afraid to listen to it.

It was cold under the tarpaulin, colder than I had ever been in my life. Yet, I wished I could remove the plastic sheet from over our heads. I wished I could see the stars of my homeland one last time. I wished I could breathe the free air.

I didn't know it then, but Devdas's vengeance was waiting for me upstairs.

The first time I set foot in my second home, it was disappointing, to say the least. I had never seen so much, and so little, at the same time. Paharganj, my mother said. Yet, I could see no mountains. Names were deceptive.

The thugs from the *akhada* were waiting for me, righteous purpose in their eyes. I had seen that look in the eyes of my mother's pimps when she did what she did. I knew what was about to follow. I knew now, the last thing she saw.

They were waiting for us, the pimps and the madams. It didn't take them long to understand that we were running, that we were lost, and the law had fucked us. There was righteous purpose in their eyes. They had Work for my mother. And when I was older and prettier, they'd have Work for me.

I couldn't bring myself to run. I couldn't bring myself to flinch. One of them held up the 'Free Kashmir' pamphlets, along with 'Inquilaab' calls from the JNU protest. Another held the mask I had worn that day.

This was Devdas's parting gift.

I heard the largest of them mutter one word, spit it out of his tongue like the seed of a bad fruit, and I knew that my fate was sealed.

'*Azaadi* … eh?'

As the assault started, I thought of a whore, beaten for helping her daughter. They beat me like one, too, indifferent to my flesh since it was rotten anyway. A whore's death all the way. No one to mourn me, no one to remember. Like never having existed.

As agony hit me on all sides, I knew why the old lady had said that my mother wasn't really dead. She was very much alive, by my side, screaming through me, closer to me than she had been in years.

And I finally understood why Devdas was addicted to pain.

19

COWARD

Devdas

Whores, beggars, outlaws, gypsies. Can you pick the odd one out? It's tricky, isn't it? To pick the odd one out among all the odd ones. On the other hand, it's easy to see how they're all similar. Not that they are all odd, no. They are all unwanted. The dregs of civilization. Offensive by definition. Like the loud, wheezing, fat clerk in a cramped bus. You know they exist; you just wish they didn't.

It does something to your mind, being unwanted. What, you ask? Well, something. I had first-hand experience, and even I couldn't tell you exactly *what*. That's the first conscious thought I remember having, the day my mother disappeared. That's the last sane thought I remember having, the day I saw the whore with my father.

What happens when that happens? I can't tell you *exactly*, but think I'll take a guess.

It all becomes about being wanted again. What you say, what you think, how you look, everything designed to make sure no one leaves you again. You say what they want to hear, you look the way they'd like to see you, you *think* like they want you to think. So that's what I did, most of my life. Rode the wave of the zeitgeist and a few chicks along the way. *They* wanted me all right.

Until the day I was caught screaming at my sister for wanting to sleep with someone other than me.

They knew me for the fraud I was,
they knew I wasn't who I said I was.

Like a house of cards, it all came tumbling down. Unlike a house of cards, it didn't collapse with a little whoosh, but with a bit of a phweeee. There was outrage. The Professor's son, using his privilege to intimidate little girls, while pretending to be one of *them*.

They no longer wanted me, my poetry, my protests, my voice. All for the simple act of pretending to be something I was not. Riddle me this: who amongst you isn't pretending to be something you're not? Who amongst you doesn't start believing it a little?

The metamorphosis happens without your knowledge, behind your back. You live in a Kafkaesque world, believing you're human. The truth is too horrific to face. For you are just a giant bug. Ugly, on your back, a dozen legs flailing in the air, with a shell for a cocoon.

That's who the whore embraced in that seedy cinema hall. A bug.

My mouth was bleeding when I took my seat. My tongue played with a loosened tooth, and the sweet ache put a smile on my face. It made me oblivious to all memory and sensations, so it took a while to realize that Chandramukhi was sobbing next to me. Maybe it was the film. I had seen the gaudy poster outside. It warranted tears.

Even crying, she brought comfort to me, knowing she was right there. It had been weeks since I had started staying at her shack. I didn't know why she suffered a bug like me, nor did I know what she wanted. Until now.

She wanted me.

As she planted a flurry of impatient, hungry kisses all over my face, I knew I was a comfort to her, as well. She climbed the peak and embraced all of me.

I hadn't experienced sex like this before. I imagined this was what it would have been like with Paro. For a while, I wasn't the child whose mother had run off with the cable guy, nor was I the boy who disfigured his sister. For a while, there was nothing to prove.

I don't know how long we sat there after I finished, with Chandramukhi slumped over me. I did know that my wounds were starting to hurt again. They were no longer welcome.

Her love gave me a bit of courage, but not enough to tell her about what I had done to Paro. No, all love was conditional, and I didn't think hers could stand the truth.

I'd do the next-best thing my newfound courage allowed me the temerity to do.

I'd confess my sins to my sister.

I half-hoped I wouldn't find her at the house. That I would get a practice run with the Professor. I'd be no more a disappointment than his own father was. Saying it out loud would prepare me to face Paro.

Nothing could prepare me for what I was about to find.

As I peeked into my father's study, I heard a mirthful, derisive sound. A woman's laugh. More hard-earned and intimate than an orgasm in a cheap theatre.

Chandramukhi.

'He hasn't been in too much trouble, has he?' my father asked her.

'I think I made a breakthrough today,' she replied, pleased with herself. 'I think I will be all the trouble he can handle for a while.'

Further cackling. A whore's laugh. More merciless and damaging than a beating in an *akhada*.

'Keep taking care of him, will you?'

'I will, Professor.' She stood up to leave. 'And I thank you for everything you've done for me–I don't know where I would've landed up had it not been—'

'Nonsense. You had talent. I just gave it an outlet.'

Was he smirking as he said it? I couldn't tell. I imagined he did. I imagined *all* her talent.

He continued, still with that maybe-smirking face, 'What you've done for Devdas. You've paid me back plenty.'

So, that's why she had taken me in. As a favour to a customer. Did he pay her to screw me? Keep me too busy to throw acid at sleeping girls? Did he already know?

I didn't stop and eavesdrop any longer. I was afraid, more than I had been in a long time. That familiar feeling of the ego crying. That righteous anger clawing its way to my fingernails. I was afraid I might do it again. I had hurt Paro; I was capable of hurting Chandramukhi.

I had to run.

First, though, I needed an outlet for *my* talent. I needed someone to hurt so I wouldn't hurt her. Before I knew it, I was in the *akhada* once again, gouging out an eye of one of the oily beasts. Before they knew it, I was gone.

Back in Chandramukhi's shack, I packed whatever little I had accumulated over the past weeks. I stuffed my stuff in a polythene bag, spared a glance at her favourite book, and scampered off. This was goodbye.

I didn't know it then, but a battalion of Hulks was headed my way, seeking retribution. Not for the gouged eye, no, but for being a caste-traitor. The *pehelwaans* knew where I hung out. They had teased me about the whore. So, they knew where to find me. See, I was the next best thing to Chunnilal.

My Spirit Animal had published his article. I don't know how to explain what he did next. Maybe he didn't know the power of the Serif. Maybe he felt immune to its consequences. Maybe he simply didn't care.

Why else would he forward them the link to his fucking website?

I would narrowly miss them. Chandramukhi wouldn't. They waited for her there, and I waited for my bus at Kashmiri Gate. Once upon a time, the terminus was the start of a road that led to the Valley, *her* home, but it offered more destinations now.

I wasn't going to a place I knew;
I was going to a place I had sworn never to.

That's when she called, at the most unsuitable moment, when I was considering the hellish journey next to the uncouth, *paan*-spitting masses. I spat at her too, all the slaked lime I could muster. I hoped it stung her as bad as it cut my tongue.

I bought my ticket and waited for the bus. The last one had left thirty-six hours ago, and the next one wouldn't leave for another twelve. The name of the town I was going to wasn't written anywhere on a chart. It wasn't anywhere you wanted to go. It wasn't on the way to anywhere you wanted to go.

It was a place you went to start over. A place professors' wives and cable guys could disappear in.

A place a boy could go to see his mother.

20
ETHER

Paro

What's the rupee value of misery, I have often wondered.

They have specialists for everything else out there. Stocks, currency, websites, intellectual property, ad spots, the telecom spectrum. All intangible, all born out of a collective will to agree on the existence of something that doesn't, actually.

Pain exists, misery is real. How is its worth calculated in a country where it's manufactured and subsidised and delivered to every man, woman, and child?

When the last one of us—the lowest, the poorest, the most disabled—is as miserable as the rest of us, *that* is when we stop striving for a better world. No one left behind. The Mahatma said that, I think.

If you say enough things like that, they make movies on you. They made one on the Mahatma. One scene had three lakh extras. For the longest time, I couldn't believe it. I mean, who did the counting? How would one know where one person ends and the other begins?

I wonder how many of them were as miserable as the man playing the Mahatma, following his salty steps. What was the worth of their misery? Not much, I guess. They were playing extras in someone else's story. Most of us are. I was.

In the Mukherjee household, I had misery pegged pretty good early on. A dozen blisters on my hands meant enough *sarkanda* for two-thirds of a bowl of rice. Three smacks from Dev *bhaiya* translated into a balcony ticket at the cinema. A cheeky answer to the Professor meant a new chore.

The math was simple enough to be understood by a child. I don't know why I couldn't understand it now.

In a country with a rape every fifteen minutes—sorry, a *reported* rape every fifteen minutes—it's strange how some cause an outrage and some don't. How does the news producer know which to showcase on primetime, and which to hide? How do they know which will make the audience *care*?

A minister rapes a minor for years. The audience doesn't care. An FIR is filed, she's intimidated and her family killed.

It doesn't care, no, not yet. They burn her. Kill her, too, *and* her lawyer for good measure. The audience reads the snippets, each crueller than the last. And it grows numb and number. It insulates itself with a layer of placenta, back into its mother's womb. Deluding itself that this is an anomaly, that this can't happen to them. They *know* that's bullshit. The minister's just not focused on them yet.

Then one day, something snaps, something arbitrary. And in a country full of beheadings and hangings and lynchings, the inevitably numb and wilfully dumb audience decides to give a shit. The news producer picks up on the ratings, and puts a price-tag on the misery.

The primetime ad slot. That's the value of misery. They have specialists to do the math.

Someone did the math for Chandramukhi. Something about her made the audience feel something. A Jamia student was assaulted in Paharganj, the haunt of the loveless. Beaten, probably raped. Fighting for her life, in a medically-induced coma.

The paparazzi went to the trouble of breaking into Chandramukhi's hospital room and clicking pictures, tubes sticking out of her like a many-handed Goddess. And then those divine megapixels were sold to primetime, screenshotted and shared on sweet ol' internet.

That's where I heard about her. The Burns Unit had too much burnt flesh and not enough bandages to go around. What they did have was wi-fi. I could take a trip out of my own misery, into everyone else's. There they were: idiots, putting their thoughts on to the digital ether, thinking that someone cared.

A picture of a mob dragging a woman by the hair. '*Today I lost my faith in humanity.*'

The portrait of a girl sitting in her college campus, the sun over-exposing her face to appear a couple of shades fairer. She didn't have a right to refer to herself in the third person; she was neither the Prime Minister, nor a house-elf. She did it anyway. '*She's graceful, and eternally grateful, for the sun-kissed days.*'

A video of a man feeding a hungry dog. '*Today I regained my faith in humanity.*'

And then there was that picture of Chandramukhi, that had made people feel something. I recognized her, but barely. There were bandages on her limbs, and a hashtag over her face. *#JusticeForChandramukhi. No true Indian will scroll down without liking this post, or you'll have bad luck in your life for the next twenty years.*

I must've seen it at birth and just scrolled away.

Seventeen thousand two hundred and ninety-three shares. Thirty-six thousand four hundred and seven retweets. They all wanted justice. They didn't mind splashing her broken body on display to do that. They needed others to *feel* as well.

What did I feel? For a while, nothing. It was that numbness all over again. The shell that insulated me from the misery of others. It had for years, and it would continue to do so for the rest of my life.

This moment, though, was the interlude. I was bloodthirsty.

The nurses in my ward were whispering, excited, a little irritated. The girl from Paharganj had been brought here. They were saying she was a prostitute. What did she expect would happen? You live by the dick, you die by the dick.

They were preparing me for surgery, the third since it happened. I wasn't drugged yet, but my head was spinning. I asked them where Chandramukhi was being kept, and the whispers let me in on the secret.

I excused myself to go to the bathroom, and took my bandaged self through the antiseptic corridors. I followed the trail of policemen, who knew the value of the primetime ad slot was more than their jobs. They needed to get a head on their spike.

Outside Chandramukhi's room, an inspector was scratching his head, leaning into a lady constable.

'... a customer, you think?'

The lady constable shook her head. 'She wasn't a worker there. The madam confirmed it. She was just a college student making a documentary.'

'Fuck. This just gets worse. I liked her better when she was a prostitute. Anything else?'

'The last thing the girl said—'

'Yeah, yeah ... but it seems like a weird thing to say. You sure you heard it right. *Devdas*?'

The lady constable nodded. 'Yes, sir. Right before they put her under, that's what she said. *Devdas*. I think she was telling us who did this to her.'

'That'd make sense, but *Devdas*?' the inspector was getting pissed. 'Who do I arrest? Bloody Shahru—?'

Neither of them had been paying attention to me. Even in hospitals, people avoid people in bandages like the plague. I stepped in closer, until they no longer could.

'I think I can help you, Inspector.'

I told them everything. His number. His real name. I even called him up so that they could triangulate his location. They caught him fast asleep on a distinguished wooden bench at the Bus Terminus, preparing to flee the city.

Devdas had done it once. He had done it twice. There wouldn't be a third time. I had repaid my debt to the Professor. Now I had to repay my debt to *her*.

The last thing I ever heard Devdas say to me was, 'Hello ... hello ... Paro?'

I just hoped he learnt the value of misery.

21

ALL HER TALENT

Chandramukhi

Did you judge me, like Devdas did? It was easy for him to believe that I was a whore. Like my mother. Or his. Was it easy for you, too?

I guess I haven't been completely truthful. I guess some memories are too painful to share. I guess it doesn't matter now.

'*... after that, after that she had no chance. She was ... disappeared.*'

That's what the old lady had said. After what? I didn't ask, for I knew what she meant. What my mother had done, no pimp could forgive her for it.

Some lives are meant to be examples. Hers was. She was an example of what happened to the wives of terrorists. She ended up being an example of what happened to those ungrateful for their pimp's generosity.

I was thirteen. The only reason that I wasn't already Working was because my mother's pimp was a man of principles. But he had waited long enough and could wait no more. Not when there was money to be made.

The day they came for me was like any other day. Innocuous, no more treacherous than the one before it. My mother sensed it, in their eyes and in their gaits. When you make your living trying to get men to voice and commit to their deepest, darkest desires, it's not that difficult to see through their facades.

She helped me run away. They caught her, of course. I heard her screams as I ran from the men pursuing me. She fought like a demon, wailed like a banshee, did everything she could to give me a fighting chance.

It was sudden. I didn't know where to go, whom to go to. I could have gone back for her, but I was afraid of the thin, tired, sweaty men that came to visit her dimly-lit room every night. I was old enough to notice that they noticed me. That the blacks of their eyes grew blacker when they rested on me.

I wandered the streets, which were full of thin, sweaty men, very much expecting to be taken back to a dimly-lit room echoing with the sound of clap-clap-clap. Yet, I needed to help my mother. And I knew of someone scarier than pimps—the Uniforms.

I saw a Uniform and tapped him gently on his clean, clenched *khaki* ass. He turned around, frowning at me. I wanted to run, wilting under his gaze. Yet, his eyes were kind and inquisitive. They noticed me. They told me I could ask for his help. And I did.

It didn't help. My mother and my pursuers were far gone. And I had never been allowed to wander the streets by myself. I had no idea what to tell the policeman. We did walk the streets for hours in futility, and at the end, he made me a promise. He'd keep looking, while I remained under the care of the Sisters of the Church.

The Sisters were strict, but I knew what turned them on. I memorized my Bible, read my verses, cleaned up after myself. They had uniforms, too, and I knew nothing pleased Uniforms more than obedience. As for the Uniform who made me that promise, he never came back.

I stopped looking for my family and I survived. She didn't … and she didn't.

I wasn't bothered about my future, because I knew I didn't have one, or at least, not a say in it. The fate of abandoned kids like me was more or less certain. We were too old to be adopted, and too young to make sensible decisions. Boys were better off, but then they always are. Most girls, though, would end up being a Contraption, just another household item to make other people lazy. Some would end up in dimly-lit rooms.

Everyone dreaded their eighteenth birthday. Everyone knew what awaited us. We were tasteless, rotten morsels of the world, spit into these orphanages. Now we'd be spit back to be chewed some more, to see if the flavour was any better. But time never cured a rotten fruit, it only made it worse.

Once in a blue moon, a girl developed a talent. Something that stood out. Something that could save her.

For me, it was stories. They had been the only escape in Paharganj, before my actual escape. Dirty, seedy theatres full of sweaty, skinny men. My mother and I would find a corner away from the blowjobs and the handjobs, find joy in misery not our own.

Horror. Revenge. Melodrama. Devotional. Action. I watched it all. I experienced every single emotion in that cinema hall, before I experienced all of them together as I made love to my Devdas.

I picked up a knack for telling a story, which brought me to the attention of his father. It was at the vocational school. Before I turned eighteen, I needed to learn to fend for myself, if I didn't want to be a Contraption. Time was running out, and I was furiously trying to learn how to sew garments, so I did not have to spend a lifetime laundering them.

The fancy Professor had come to visit us underprivileged folks. His revolutionary days were long behind him. But there was still a mad glint in his eyes when he spoke about the dignity of labour.

After he was done speaking to us about us, he spoke to the volunteers about us. He was looking for someone who stood out. Someone who wouldn't be ignored. We were all unique, he was told, all special, all talented. He chuckled at that. Then he called me.

'You want to tell stories, I've heard,' he asked me. 'What kind, may I ask?'

'I don't know. All kinds. My own. My mother's.'

'And why do you want to tell it?'

'I don't know ...'

He did not accept that answer.

'Why do you want to tell it?'

'Because people ought to know.'

He picked me.

I do not know why. Why should he care that this girl wanted to tell stories? Why would he put her through college? I didn't ask, *why me?*

I had asked that question my entire life. When Kashmir took my father. When Paharganj took my mother. Over and over, with no answer. So, when the Professor came into my life, generous and too good to be true, I didn't ask, *why me*? I asked something else, something that made more sense at the time.

Why *not* me?

That we ended up in each other's arms wasn't something he meant for to happen. No matter what the Professor believed, it didn't happen because he wanted it. It happened because I did.

He paid for my graduation. I paid for my camera-phone. And my camera-phone paid for my post-graduation.

I turned into a stringer. A scavenger. Looking for scraps of gore to sell as photos and videos. Most of the work happened in the night, when real journalists were sound asleep with their families. It was me and my scooter, heading from crime scene to road accident to fire break-outs.

I didn't need the Professor by the time I started my mass communications course from Jamia. Not in the financial sense, no. I just needed someone who knew me. And since we had first spoken, Narayan Mukherjee somehow did.

It wasn't like there weren't other Men, some boys, and a couple of girls. It was just that none of them understood that I was missing a part. One I was yet to go and find.

It was the second year of my master's degree. They asked us to make a documentary film. I knew it was time.

When I rented out a shack in Paharganj, the Professor didn't ask me not to go. He knew I had to. That had been the purpose all along. To help me tell the story of my mother. It was me and my camera-phone in the streets, trying to find her, recording my encounters, my clues, my memories.

I named my film before I finished it.

The Search.

And one day, I bumped into him. My very own sad, lost Devdas.

The reason why I hid my truth from him, why I let him think I screwed people for money, was not because I wanted him to be Devdas. It was simply because I wanted to be Chandramukhi.

It was just a story. It was supposed to be just a story.

'Congratulations, miss. They got him.'

Never knew that my eyelids could hurt. Yet there they were, hurting as I pulled them open. The nurse who had whispered the words into my ear suddenly jumped back, alarmed that I was awake.

She turned to call the doctor, but I grabbed her hand, with my hurting left one.

'Who?'

She winked at me. '*Devdas*.'

For a moment, nothing. A state of oblivion. Then panic.

'What—why? Who said—?' I tried to sit up but her firm hand kept me in place.

'You mentioned his name before you went under … they found him trying to flee the city. Don't worry. The police put him exactly where he belongs.'

'No …' my voice was weak, unconvincing, 'he didn't do anything.'

Of course, he had not *done* anything. He wouldn't want to sully his hands beating me. No, all he had done was send his comrades from the *akhada* to my door. Telling them what he'd found in my room. Telling them he knew where to find one of those masked bitches from the JNU protest.

You know what? I didn't care. It didn't change what I felt about my Devdas, what I needed from him. There should have been shame in admitting that, but I had none.

My love was illogical. My love came before self-preservation. My love didn't demand some back in return. All it required was someone to bury my dead body, someone to cry a little, someone to remember me. Devdas may not be able to give me much, but at least he could save me from the ignominy of an unmarked grave.

I thought of my poor Devdas in his poor little jail cell.

I called the Uniforms to my side. They seemed to care enough to come this time. I gave them the lie. Devdas was not to blame. They believed it. Or pretended to.

But even an innocent man in jail must wait for the paperwork to catch up with his innocence. In this country, that takes almost as much time as it takes for eighteen fractures, a ruptured spleen, and two surgeries to come to a successful close.

Both Devdas and I ended our sentences together. There was no one waiting for me outside the hospital when I left, and I was determined that there would be someone to greet Devdas when he got out. I reached Tihar an hour earlier than I was supposed to. It had taken my father in its deep, hungry bowels. Now it held my lover.

There was sudden pandemonium inside. Almost as if they knew I would be returned to the boy I loved. Yet, I was almost inconsequential; no one seemed to have time enough to tell me anything. Something had happened. Something out of the ordinary, as ordinary as ordinary can be in jail.

I saw him. A cake of dried blood over the right-half of his face. Being wheeled off on a gurney to the morgue. No longer hateful. No longer tormented.

My lovely, dead Devdas. Privileged, even in death.

For I would mourn him, but who would mourn me?

22

NOT IN MY NAME

Devdas

I died a junkie. That's who I was when my head got bashed in. Being one wasn't *per se* what got me killed, though. That was something different. Something out of my control. I was killed by a fucking typo.

It's a relief, honestly, though, dying. No, I am not being facetious. Just take a look around you. This place is a goddamned travesty. This capitalist utopia riding the bigoted hair of the Fuhrer's moustache. Who wouldn't rather be dead?

It's not like I'd be missing much. A mother who didn't want anything to do with me, a father who didn't want anything to do with me. A girl who hated me, another girl who hated me. A bunch of strangers who'd cheer if the lawmen put a bullet in me.

What about children, though? Mini-Devs strutting around the place. Oh God, children. Is there anything more selfish a man can do than subject a human being to this world, or the world to another human being? Knowing what's in store for both? Nah. They're better off not existing at all.

It's strange, the thought of ceasing to exist. Nothing on the other side. No memory. No consciousness. Zilch. Full stop. It's even stranger, that despite its inevitability, the fear of death doesn't paralyze or madden you more often.

Have you seen monkeys going batshit—no, apeshit—crazy some days? Scratching their hair and dangling their balls and throwing shit at each other? Maybe they are smarter than us, maybe they know about the futility of life. They just have a more sensible reaction to it than we do.

That's what I spent my life doing. Scratching my hair and dangling my balls and throwing shit. Was it sensible, enlightened? Well, let me just say it ended with those around me having shit-stained faces.

In jail, I wasn't the only one flinging.

I guess I should thank my father for me being in this particular jail, or the government clerk who made the typo. The latter for making the mistake, and the former for not correcting it. It didn't matter, see. At least not to my father. Age was just a number. He had the bourgeoisie to overthrow. Students to screw. A kid to ignore.

And so, the typo stayed. On paper, I was eighteen years old. Had my father bothered to get it corrected, I would be with a less brutal class of criminals. I would be in juvenile prison. I would be seventeen. And alive.

Aah well. Maybe I have missed the point as completely as a pair of debating theologians. Maybe there *is* no God. Maybe there are no coincidences. Maybe I did die from being a junkie.

I could bear the pain of hating Chandramukhi, of leaving her behind. As long as she still loved me, wanted me. What I couldn't bear, was her hating me. And then they had to tell me what had happened to her, what I had caused to happen.

Of course, she hated me. Of course, she blamed me. As did Paro. As did I. All of us, united and shit-stained to boot. Chandramukhi had told the policemen who I was, given up my name. That's how they caught me. That's how I knew.

The Inside wasn't that different from the real world. Despite all of us being criminals, some criminals were better than others. Despite all of us being in it together, most hated most. What you *did* determined who you'd *be*. And in that ladder, anti-nationals occupied the lowest rung, followed by paedophiles, followed by rapists.

That's where they thought I belonged. The third-lowest rung. They had seen the news, so they felt informed. I had hurt that poor little girl, how could I have resisted the urge to rape her? They already had ample reason to hate me. I was about to give them an excuse to act upon it.

I walked up to the men who traded in contraband on the Inside. The Haves. The bourgeoisie. The ones who could kill another inmate and not pay for it.

I walked up to them, mean-looking bastards all, and taunted them.

As the first blow paraded through my flesh and bone, I felt the bliss of nothingness. Oh, there was pain, all right. Enough of it to free me from everything else. No guilt, no ambition, no Chandramukhi, no Paro.

Just one sane thought in my head.

Make it stop.

It wouldn't, thankfully. I had lit the fuse, knowing full well what I was getting into. This was no ten-second fight. This was not the *akhada*, self-contained and safe. This was the Inside. This was relapse.

In here, when a junkie hurt for his next fix, chances were that he'd overdose on it. My itch was scratched now. There'd be nothing to want any more. There'd be no more feeling unwanted.

So, good luck to you. Congratulations on inheriting this world. Keep it. Just leave me out of it. And whichever schmuck ends up telling our story, I hope you don't remember their name.

I hope you never discover mine.

23
DOMESTICATION

Paro

There is nobody more free than someone who's made their peace with the fact that the world will never know their name. That none would care or remember that they were ever even here. That their life will be a single geometrical point, illegible, indistinct in the A-B line of history.

That's why the unfit and underpaid uncles of the world, travelling in buses, taking the locals, don't care what anyone thinks of them. They know, in their heart of hearts, that no one thinks of them. They don't mind if you see them fingering their nose or scratching their armpit. They know that their faces will be forgotten.

All that's real is the fleeting pleasure of scratching that itch.

'My dear child, just tell me what you need and I'll make it happen,' he asked me. The low, hushed tone and the creased forehead were almost convincing. Looking at him, I almost believed he was talking to me, and not to the paid reporter recording our interaction.

I wasn't worth primetime. Acid attacks were much too common, and no news honcho had been sufficiently moved by my plight. They weren't the only vultures out there, though. One hovered over my hospital bed, complete with the trademarked politician's cap and an XL vermillion *tilak*.

'I thank you, Mr MLA, sir, but there really isn't anything ...' I croaked back. I, too, was almost convincing, when I said, 'I want nothing from you.'

Scavengers don't like it when the carcass has a choice. His brow creased further.

'But—but I am the Chair of our party's Women's Welfare Wing. And your life ... has been destroyed so completely by this heinous act. We'd like to help you start anew ... get you married, maybe?'

It seemed clear that he believed he'd just offered me the moon. Pfft. I had the stars in mind.

'Well ... if you really can, I'd appreciate some help with this artisan group I represent. We are a bunch of low-income *muddha*-makers from Haryana. You don't suppose you could ... maybe ... get us a permanent vendor space somewhere in Delhi? Maybe the INA market?'

The MLA stared at me in wonder, only now comprehending that there were two vultures in the room. The reporter clicked a photograph and scribbled furiously.

'I mean ... since my life is all but over, I'd like to help my people the best I can ... maybe even join your—what was it, the women's thing?—somewhere down the line.'

The MLA broke out in a huge smile. Of course, he'd help me do this. That's what he was here for.

And just like that, I was an owner. That was *my* itch. Devdas had never been *mine*, so to speak, except inside my head. I drank from the bottle, but my lips had never dared touch it. For the bottle was borrowed.

There were others like me, who had been owned all their lives. The artisans from my erstwhile home. Poor. Powerless. Domesticated through generations of co-dependence with their owners. They got food and a chance to breed. The masters got obedience, and the next generation of trained sheep.

It was time for a change of ownership. I knew what I was about to do would piss Bhuvan off. He had been the master for so long, he'd not react well to his livestock, his artisans being snatched from under his nose. There was nothing he could do about it, though. He was the one who had insisted on having no written agreement with the people we dealt with. He couldn't claim their services now.

No contract, no case.

The law screwed everyone. It was just Bhuvan's time.

As for the livestock, they wouldn't technically be free, but I'd make sure they had a little more food and a bit more sex. If I was to be an owner, I'd have to act like one.

I needed this, to be me. More than I needed *someone*. I'd rather risk unhappiness by myself than be someone else with someone else. I knew exactly what kind of life I intended to lead, for it translated directly into the kind of death I was going for.

There are two kinds of dead people. The first are remembered—fleetingly, of course—for the things they did when they were alive. Made money. Travelled. Loved. Lost. The second are remembered for the things they did *not* do in life. Never cheated anyone. Never committed a crime. Never hurt a fly.

I hoped to avoid the second kind of death, and in turn, life. I intended to lie, cheat, be ruthless like a storm and be forgotten when I passed. I needed my life to be eventful, for in death, lay inevitable obscurity. I was fine with being forgotten, just like dear old Dev.

He may have had everything, but he needed his sorrows and pain like everyone else. Even if it meant he was the one who had to cause them. We are who we are, we do what we must do.

I am not Haryana when I am in Haryana. I am not unloved when no one loves me. I am not owned when I owe something.

I am who I am regardless of where or what I am.

24
META

Chandramukhi

The documentary on my mother didn't grab the headlines. It didn't capture film festivals. It didn't get awards. It was much too common, for it seemed that anyone who desired to create art had a whore to unclothe. Beneath the bluster, it was the same story, the same bruises, the same scars.

And it wasn't like pretty people crying in the movies, beautiful and heart-breaking. Real people were ugly, and so were their tears. A much-too-true depiction of crying isn't what the audience wanted to see. At least, not in the country I was born in; there was too much misery already.

Who *The Search* did end up appealing to was the BBC, where I was offered an internship. I had been taught about the plundering, colonial British Raj, but for the first time, I realized exactly how much wealth they'd looted. Enough to actually pay their interns.

The Professor helped me with the visa application to the UK. That was the last time I saw him. He had wanted to continue to help, to stay in touch. I promised I would, and I broke the promise. He reminded me too much of his son. Just as his son used to remind me of him.

The Professor had been a father to all three of us, but we were too dead or too far or too far gone to need him any more. Like all children, we outgrew him.

Neither I nor Paro were there when they burned Dev's body. Womenfolk aren't allowed in cremations. They aren't tough enough to bear witness to the horrific dance of flesh and flame. Ha! Try telling that to Paro.

I don't know if she would have come had she been allowed. I would have. Devdas deserved at least one woman who loved him to cry for him. He wasn't a complete monster, I suppose. He had just let some of them loose on me.

Dev was gone, so was my mother. And it was too costly to stay in touch with my father; postage stamps and international calls were beyond the means of the intern and the inmate. My Search remained unending.

I fell in love again. It was easy, and quick. I didn't mean to, I didn't expect to, but I did. Many times, with many Men.

I think I was even loved back once or twice. The names are all muddled, though.

I still had my stories, thankfully. My employer recognized that I recognized misery. So, they sent me to find them all. Victims of this, victims of that. Any hope I had, of leaving the misery behind, was left behind.

My bosses made me sign a bond like a possessive spouse, promising to not leave them for someone else. And I did. Sign the bond, that is, hand upon my heart. They sent me to the far edges of London, then the UK, then Europe. A dog on a leash, being offered a longer leash, being trained to always come back. And I always came back. For I had grown accustomed to my kennel. There was no other home to go to.

It was a mildly abusive relationship, but it wasn't like I had the luxury of choice.

It wasn't until six years after I joined them that they let the leash loose enough for me to do a story in India. I knew it well, they thought. And by now, it would be alien enough for me to dutifully return.

Besides, I knew the victim.

She was leading a revolution of sorts, organizing oppressed communities into little blocks of self-funded, self-operated LLPs, leveraging their skills against a global market. Artisans, innovators, food processors, truckers. A contrarian of sorts, she was on Forbes 30 under 30 last year, and was addressing the UNESCO conference in Delhi this year. A woman who'd faced insurmountable odds, personal tragedy, a savage attack, but refused to cower down. She was younger than me, but had done so much more. I'd have normally resented that, but not when it came to her.

Dear ol' Paro.

The world is only as evolved as the stories of its time. And Paro had a pretty sick story, if I do say so myself. It had heartbreak, betrayal, and triumph. The audience lapped it up, especially the triumph. Because that is the story we tell ourselves. That she won. The she prevailed. That she found love. Of course, it's not true.

It wasn't always like that. They used to tell the tales of gods and their wars. Mahabharat, Ramayan, Iliad, Odyssey. Their stories were of right and wrong. Not any more. These days they tell stories of women who triumph. It doesn't matter who's right, it matters who wins.

Paro won. She didn't take shit lying down. She screwed the system. And anyone who knew her story believed that the system could be screwed. That's how evolved the audience is.

The Professor would've been proud of her rabble-rousing.

'You still carrying around that thing?'

Her voice was different than I remembered, though I didn't remember her voice.

'Hello, Paro.' I closed the copy of *Devdas* I was reading, the copy I had had since when I had more family than I had lost.

Paro simply took the book out of my hands without asking for permission. I guess she was used to it by now. An Owl stared back at her from the back cover. She ran her finger over *Devdas*'s tattered spine, touching its world and stories and characters.

'Just some light reading.' My voice broke her trance, and she handed my book back to me.

'I am sorry to have kept you waiting,' she smiled, 'I was firefighting.'

She plonked down on the sofa next to me, her faded scars catching the light in a way that made them look like wrinkles. She pointed at my bag where I had unceremoniously stuffed the book.

'Why read something over and over? Why not pick up something new?'

'It's familiar …' I shrugged, and added, 'and I guess I always felt a kinship with Chandramukhi.'

'Maybe you just don't want it to be over?'

I smiled. She was much too smart to accept anything except the truth.

'It's like a relationship, a book,' I mumbled, hoping it sounded less sentimental that way. 'You live it with the characters. It's literally just words, ink on paper, so you *build* what words don't. It might be someone else's reality, but it's *your* world. You design the details, you decide the colours, you decipher the language.'

'And then it ends …'

'It's like someone close to you died.' And I had enough of that already. 'What about you? You ever felt like that?'

Paro looked flummoxed with the question, and I imagined she wasn't flummoxed by many things.

'I don't know, not really,' then she smiled, as though remembering something, 'there was a poem, though, in school. *Rashmirathi*. Used to love that. Haven't read it in years.'

'That's the Mahabharat from the point of view of the—'

'The illegitimate son, yes. The one who wasn't supposed to exist, who's gifted to his mother by the Sun-God. And fearing for her reputation, she gives him up, to be raised by others.'

It didn't surprise me that the story appealed to her, but it surprised me that she chose to share it.

'There was something about the tragic hero that got me ... he was raised as a poor man, and then someone offered a hand of friendship, showed him generosity. And the rest of his life, he sought to repay that kindness, even going against his own family, paying with his life. It used to make sense to me, now I don't seem to get it, why he did that.'

'I thought he felt that was the honourable thing. To repay the favour?'

'That's it, though. If it wasn't his fault that he was born deprived and in debt, why should he be grateful for some good fortune?'

I didn't have an answer for that, and I told her so. She didn't either. We sat in silence for a while, ruing our non-answers.

I knew, like you somehow do, that it was the end of small talk. Like a book in your hands nearing its end. The two halves of the book, the one that you've read, and the one that you still have to, have grown unequal. And you're left holding the thinner end …

It's come to this, without the story having reached a satisfying conclusion. You hope there is one more surprise, one more twist to make it all worth it, but there isn't. It's the end, and you've given a piece of yourself to it that you won't get back, and you've taken a piece of it with you, which you can't give up.

But I wasn't ready, this wasn't a fair trade. This couldn't be all that I had to say to Paro, to ask her. If the silence grew longer, it would last forever.

'Why did you do it, Paro?' I finally blurted out the question I had wanted to ask her for six years. 'Why did you give them Dev's name?'

She stared at me coldly. 'You know why.'

'I—know—why,' my frustration spat each syllable separately. 'But—but *why*? Why did you have to do it?' It wasn't a question for her, but the cosmos. Maybe she understood that, for her eyes grew softer.

'Because you wouldn't have. You were blind. And like most of us, you chose your blindness. It wouldn't have let you see him, *truly* see him.'

I knew she was right, yet it felt like she had stolen something precious from me.

'I couldn't even say goodbye …' *Again.* What I'd give to say goodbye, just once.

'Does it really matter?'

'What?' I couldn't believe even she could be so cruel.

'Does the last thing you said to a person really matter? The ones who are dead are dead. They don't dwell on it. And you … don't you have better memories to dwell on?'

I nodded, dissipating the wetness on my eyelashes by blinking really fast. It was instinctual for me, I guess, to first agree with someone and then actually think about the thing they said. Once I did, I realized what she was doing.

She wasn't trying to be cruel. In her own weird way, I think she was trying to make me feel better.

'Why?'

'What?'

'Why … be kind?' I knew enough about her to know that she wasn't, by default.

She turned sheepish, which didn't suit her. It reminded me of the young little first-year, standing outside the college gates, genuinely surprised at having been barred from entering.

'Maybe because we've shared things …'

'Like?'

'A scooter ride in night-time Delhi.'

'And?'

'A ride in the Professor's car.'

Yes, I couldn't forget that. She was screaming. We were in the backseat, her face melting in my lap.

'And—'

'And …'

She spoke his name, but I couldn't hear it.

The conversation ended. We had nothing left to say to each other, except goodbye.

'Goodbye, Paro.'

'Goodbye, Chandramukhi.'

As I left, I hoped to never see her again. It would be nice to have one real goodbye.

ACKNOWLEDGEMENTS

To Shridhar sir, for being my teacher, mentor, and friend. For showing me that stories don't occur in a vacuum, but the real world. If I can be half the writer he is, I'll be twice as good as I ever hoped to be.

To Ambar, Hemali, and A Suitable Agency, for their expert guidance and unending support at every step of the way. Especially Ambar, who takes my frantic calls, fields my stupid questions, and patiently schools me in publishing.

To Prerna Gill, for the care and respect she gives to the written word; it is rare in our time, and getting rarer still. For ensuring the integrity and the vision of this story remained uncompromised.

To HarperCollins, for giving this book a home alongside the works of a pantheon of authors I admire.

And you, dear reader, the reason for it all...

ABOUT THE AUTHOR

Aayush Gupta holds an MA in English Literature from Kirori Mal College, and a BA (Hons) in Journalism from Maharaja Agrasen College, University of Delhi. Under his banner, Guddi Productions, he's directed documentary series on Indian handicrafts and rural innovations for India's public broadcaster, Prasar Bharati. His debut novel, *Toppers*, a YA political thriller, was published in 2016. Subsequently, he's worked as a screenwriter in multiple writers' rooms, writing over twenty-five episodes of Sony's iconic *C.I.D.* He's also the writer of Yash Raj Films' *The Railway Men*.

You can write to him at aayush.kaamshaam@gmail.com